Lida Mae stopped and looked at her sisters.

"Marry Tom? Not if he was the last man in Ohio!"

Suddenly, Priscilla and Rhoda's eyes widened in alarm, but before Lida Mae could turn around to see what was behind her, a deep voice bit out, "I don't recall asking you."

Closing her eyes, Lida Mae sent up a prayer that when she turned around, Tom Fisher wouldn't be standing there, having overheard their conversation.

Steeling herself, she turned around. Tom's brown eyes were narrowed to slits as he glared at Lida Mae.

"Don't worry, Lida Mae, I wouldn't marry you if you were the last girl in Texas!" Tom looked at the bag he was carrying, and thrust it into Lida Mae's hands. "Now, if you'll excuse me, I've got to get back to doing the job you want, but can't have, and that I don't want, and have no choice but to do!"

He turned and stalked off down the sidewalk, leaving the three sisters staring at his stiffly retreating back.

Anne Blackburne, award-winning newspaper columnist and best-selling author of Amish romance, has a personal motto: Never give up! This has served her well in life, and in her writing career. She lives and works in SE Ohio and is the proud mother of five grown children and one wonderful grandson. For fun she enjoys kayaking, reading, community theater and time with friends, family and her spoiled rescue poodle, Millie.

Books by Anne Blackburne

Love Inspired

Feuding with the Amish Farmer

Visit the Author Profile page at LoveInspired.com.

FEUDING WITH THE AMISH FARMER

ANNE BLACKBURNE

If you purchased this book without a cover you should be aware that this book is stolen property. It was reported as "unsold and destroyed" to the publisher, and neither the author nor the publisher has received any payment for this "stripped book."

ISBN-13: 978-1-335-62150-4

Recycling programs for this product may not exist in your area.

Feuding with the Amish Farmer

Copyright © 2026 by Anne Blackburne

All rights reserved. No part of this book may be used or reproduced in any manner whatsoever without written permission.

Without limiting the exclusive rights of any author, contributor or the publisher of this publication, any unauthorized use of this publication to train generative artificial intelligence (AI) technologies is expressly prohibited. Harlequin also exercises their rights under Article 4(3) of the Digital Single Market Directive 2019/790 and expressly reserves this publication from the text and data mining exception.

This is a work of fiction. Names, characters, places and incidents are either the product of the author's imagination or are used fictitiously. Any resemblance to actual persons, living or dead, businesses, companies, events or locales is entirely coincidental.

For questions and comments about the quality of this book, please contact us at CustomerService@Harlequin.com.

® is a trademark of Harlequin Enterprises ULC.

Love Inspired
22 Adelaide St. West, 41st Floor
Toronto, Ontario M5H 4E3, Canada
www.LoveInspired.com

HarperCollins Publishers
Macken House, 39/40 Mayor Street Upper,
Dublin 1, D01 C9W8, Ireland
www.HarperCollins.com

Printed in Lithuania

There are many devices in a man's heart;
nevertheless the counsel of the Lord, that shall stand.
—*Proverbs* 19:21

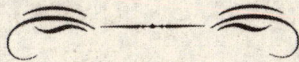

To my mother, Marian Finn Mullen, who insisted
I learned the correct usage of the English language.
You were right, Mom! It has served me well.
And the typing class you made me take, too!

Chapter One

Lida Mae Beiler put her back into her work, taking pleasure in the effort required to lift the heavy pitchfork full of soiled bedding and manure, and toss it into the waiting wheelbarrow outside the large horse stall. She rested her arms on the top of the tool for a moment, breathing in the scents of the barn; scents she loved—of horses and straw and bedding and, yes, even manure. Her black Labrador retriever, Blue, wagged her tail from where she was lying on the cool concrete floor of the corridor, letting Lida Mae know she was paying attention.

"Good girl, Blue. Almost done here, and then we'll get breakfast."

As she worked, she considered an idea she'd had for a piece of stained-glass art she'd like to design.

I think the red-and-green, double-wedding-ring-pattern quilt Maem *and my* schwestern *and I just finished would make a* wunderbar *glass quilt block. I'll see what* Maem *thinks when I'm finished here.*

Blue barked a sharp warning, and Lida Mae poked her head out of the stall. A strange young Amish man was standing a few yards down the corridor, looking at the large black dog, who was now on her feet facing him, with respect.

"It's alright, she won't hurt you," Lida Mae assured him. "Blue, sit."

The dog gave a little whine, but obeyed, and Lida reached into her pocket and pulled out a small treat, which she tossed to the dog. "*Gut* girl!" She stepped out into the corridor to run a reassuring hand over her dog's broad forehead, and turned to face the stranger fully, taking his measure.

The man looked up at her from a couple inches below her five-foot-eleven-inch height in evident surprise, but he didn't say any of the usual, tiresome things she'd heard since she was taller than most of the men in her community. He got several points for that.

"Er, *denki*. I didn't see her there in the shadows and she startled me. She's friendly?"

Lida Mae smiled at the handsome stranger, who spoke with a slight twang she found appealing. "If I tell her to be."

He raised an eyebrow. "I...see. Well, thanks for telling her, then." He stuffed his hands into the pockets of his barn coat and looked at her for several moments. "I confess, I thought you were a guy at first, but then I noticed your kerchief, and, er, other things." He gestured to her height, and she groaned inwardly. *Points lost!*

She shot him a glare. "Mmm-hmm. I get that a lot. So what can I help you with?"

His eyes widened, and he held up both hands. "I'm really sorry! I didn't mean any insult. Sure, you're tall, but you're very pretty, too!"

When she just cocked her head to the side and stared at him, he rolled his eyes and puffed out a breath. "Okay, I'm shutting up. I'm looking for Jackson Beiler. Any idea where I might find him?"

She pursed her lips. *Probably someone looking for a job. Not my business.* With a shrug, she pointed in the direction of the house. "He's probably inside the main house, getting *kaffi*."

He nodded, then gave an awkward salute. "Well, *denki* again. Um, sorry about the…"

"Don't mention it. Really," she said to forestall his apologies. Then she gave him a little wave, and pointed down the barn corridor. With a wry twist of his perfectly shaped lips, he turned and headed back the way he must have come.

Perfectly shaped lips? What's gotten into me? He's just some guy looking for a job. I'll probably never see him again, which is fine. Even if he is really handsome, and even if he was kind of cute when he embarrassed himself. Lida Mae chuckled and turned back to the stall to finish the job.

A few minutes later, she wiped her brow with the sleeve of her coveralls, exited the stall—the last in a long line of individual box stalls that made up the east wing of their brood-mare barn—and was about to push the wheelbarrow toward the manure-storage area outside the open double doors at the end of the corridor, when she heard her *dat* calling.

"Lida Mae? You in here?"

"Back here, *Dat*!" With Blue following, she dumped the cart's contents onto the manure stack in the roofed storage structure and turned to reenter the barn when her father, squinting in the bright glare of the rising sun, strode out through the double doors.

"*Ach!* There you are, *dochder*! *Gut, gut*. There's something we need to discuss."

Eyebrows raised, Lida Mae shoved her leather work gloves into the pocket of her coveralls and waited.

Jackson Beiler cast what Lida Mae might have interpreted from any other man as a nervous glance back the way he'd come. But Jackson didn't do nervous—he was way too laid-back for that. Puzzled, Lida Mae glanced toward the barn doors, but her father stepped into her line of sight and offered her a steaming mug of coffee. "Come, let's sit down."

He headed for a bench in a corner of the farmyard and lowered his six-and-a-half-foot frame, then patted the seat next to him. He gave Blue an ear rub while waiting for Lida Mae to have a seat.

Happy for a short break, Lida Mae joined her *dat* on the bench and sipped her *kaffi*, knowing he'd eventually get to the point of this impromptu meeting. Blue curled up near her feet.

Out of the corner of her eye, she saw her father stroking his full, red beard, the same penny-bright shade as her own hair. Of the three Beiler children, Lida Mae was the only one who'd inherited her *dat's* coloring. Her two sisters were both small and dark-haired like their tiny *maem*.

Lida Mae took after her father in other ways, too. In addition to her unusual height, she was also very strong, and loved working around the farm, especially with the horses her father bred and trained. She was aware that this was a point of contention between her parents. Her mother would rather Lida Mae emulate her two older sisters, who cooked and sewed, and pursued more traditionally feminine pastimes. Lida Mae could do these things competently; she simply preferred working with the horses. Her hope was that someday the farm would be hers, and she would carry on her father's tradition of raising and training fine-cart and workhorses.

Since he'd had no sons, Jackson was grateful for his daughter's capable help around the farm. Even if he didn't know the scope of her ambitions, he shouldn't be surprised to learn how much the horses and the farm meant to her.

Her father cleared his throat, a rare frown on his handsome, expressive face, and Lida Mae felt the first stirrings of anxiety. "*Dat?* What is it? Did I do something wrong? Maybe I shouldn't have turned all the broodmares out into the east field, but I really wanted to give the stalls a good cleaning, and the weather's fine, so I thought it would be alright."

He absentmindedly patted her knee. "No, no, you did nothing wrong. It's just that…well, you know how your *maem* has been fretting recently over the way you're always out here helping me in the barn, or around the farm, *ja*?"

Growing suspicious of her *dat's* motives, Lida Mae nodded. "*Ja* but, *Dat*, I always help out around the house and garden when I'm done."

He turned to face her, an almost regretful expression on his face. "I know. You're a *gut* girl, Lida Mae, and you've always been a tremendous help." He heaved a sigh. "But I can no longer let you spend your days working as if you were my son rather than my *dochder*."

Lida Mae started to speak, but her *dat* held up his big, work-roughened hand. "*Nee*, Lida Mae, it's past time. I've been unfair to you all these years, teaching you to mend fences and trim hooves and how to recognize good breeding stock. Maybe if you'd spent more time with your *maem* and *schwestern*, you'd have a beau now, and be thinking about starting a home of your own instead of wasting your time traipsing around a farm you can't hope to run by yourself after I'm gone."

Lida Mae gasped. "*Dat!* Are you sick?"

The big man gave a sad chuckle at that question. "*Ach*, no. I'm fine. But I need you to listen to me. You're a lovely *maedel*, if a bit tall. All you need is a little polish and you'll catch some young man's eye."

Starting to see red, Lida Mae struggled for calm. "I don't want to catch some young man's eye, *Dat!* I eventually want to have what you and *Maem* have—a true, deep, loving relationship. But I'm in no hurry."

He waved a hand. "*Ach*, love comes with time, child. And speaking of time, your *maem* and I agree it's time you spent more of yours learning how to become a proper Amish wife and *mudder*, not a farmer."

While she was trying to take all this in, he cast her a nervous glance before continuing. "And, well, we think you should give up puttering around with stained glass. Fancy glass art is for *Englischers*, not for us Plain folk."

Lida Mae's mouth dropped open. "*Dat!* Please, no, I love my stained glass!" She swallowed, trying to get a hold on her emotions before she burst into tears. Worried, Blue whined and pushed her cold nose into Lida Mae's hand, and she absently scratched her dog's furry cheek to let her know she was alright. She took a deep breath, knowing emotion was not the way to reach her father. "Why can't I keep on doing the stained glass?" When the words came out in a slightly guttural tone, Lida Mae cleared her throat before continuing as calmly as she could. "I love it, and I'm good at it, or they wouldn't have asked me to teach a class at the community center."

This earned another of Jackson's rare frowns. "As to that..."

"Please, *Dat*, I love working around the farm and with the horses, and I love spending my days with you." She took his large, calloused hands in her smaller, smoother ones, and met his expressive green eyes with her own, slightly damp ones of the same emerald hue. "I love making my glass quilt blocks. Besides, I still have plenty of time to find a husband. I'm only twenty! Rhoda and Priscilla are older, and you're not asking them to give up what they love, are you?"

Jackson took a moment to consider his answer. Lida Mae's sisters, Priscilla, twenty-six and widowed with a five-year-old son, and Rhoda, twenty-four and still smarting after being stood-up by her fiancé, took after their tiny, dark-haired *maem* in more than just looks. Neither of them seemed to mind filling their days with household chores, cooking and gardening, while these things bored Lida Mae.

"Well, no," Jackson hedged. "That's different."

She took a deep breath, and gave him an imploring look. "*Dat*, there's no reason I can't keep doing both—helping you out here and helping *Maem* inside. I'll get baptized and find a *mann* someday."

Jackson frowned and sat up straighter. "*Nee, dochder.* Not someday. Your *maem* and I had a discussion a few weeks ago, and, well, the fact is she finally put her foot down—"

"This is *Maem's* idea?"

Tugging at his collarless shirt as if it had grown too tight, he spoke in his most reasonable tone of voice; the one guaranteed to provoke his youngest daughter. "Now, Lida Mae. Your *mudder* only wants what's *gut* for you.

She'll have no more of you traipsing around in coveralls like a boy. She wants you in a dress like a proper young Amish *maedel*, and no more wearing coveralls and barn boots." Seeing that she was about to protest, he shook his head. "The matter is decided."

Lida Mae blinked furiously, refusing to let the angry tears filling her eyes fall. "But, *Dat*, who is going to help you around the farm?" She cleared her throat roughly. "You can't do it all by yourself, and Obadiah isn't able to carry a full workload anymore."

He shook his head sadly. "I'll miss your company, for sure and certain. But you don't need to worry about me having too much work."

She stared at him. "I don't?"

Looking pleased with himself, like a kid with a secret, he grinned. "No! Your *maem* and I figured it all out when we talked."

"You…did?"

"Oh, *ja*. Remember our old friends the Fishers?"

Trying to follow her *dat's* train of thought, she searched her memory. "Your friends in Texas?"

Her father took a deep gulp of coffee, his smile triumphant. "Exactly! They have three sons, and no daughters!"

Lida Mae thought back to their one visit to her parents' good friends in Texas. She remembered a big horse ranch, not unlike their own. And she remembered three boys; two who ran and played with them, and one who'd broken his leg, and spent a lot of time inside, reading.

Her father continued. "We talked to the Fishers, and between us, we thought up a way to solve our problem, and theirs."

She looked at him sharply. "You did?"

He nodded again. "All three sons can't inherit their

dat's spread. He doesn't want to split it up. So one, the middle son, Tom, will come here to help me out on the farm, releasing you to spend time in the house with your *maem* and sisters, doing woman stuff." He waved a vague hand in the air, indicating all the mysterious things women did. Then he gave Lida Mae a little wink. "Plus, Tom is single." He waggled his eyebrows at his bewildered daughter, and said, "Wouldn't it be perfect if one of you girls married him? Maybe this is the man for you, Lida Mae!"

Lida Mae felt panic welling up. Her voice shook with emotion as she grasped her father's arm and begged, "*Dat*, please, don't do this. Lots of women work on their farms, alongside their men or even alone. I—I was hoping you were going to leave the farm to me someday, so I could carry on the Beiler Horses tradition. Haven't I proved myself worthy? Please don't take everything I love away from me. Don't invite this boy here."

The smile fell off her father's face. "You hoped to inherit the farm and the business? Oh, Lida Mae. I didn't know. Of course, you're worthy. It isn't a question of that. But…it just isn't possible. You're a girl, no matter how big and strong you are." He looked torn for a moment, then he shook his head, his expression firming. "And, anyway, it's too late, I'm afraid. Tom's already here."

Tom Fisher stood just inside the barn, out of sight of Jackson Beiler and the woman he was currently arguing with—evidently his daughter, and probably the pretty young *maedel* he'd spoken with earlier. He was feeling very much like an intruder. He hadn't meant to eavesdrop. He'd stowed his belongings in the room Jackson had shown him in the small bunkhouse beside the sprawling barn complex, and he was simply looking for his new boss to find out what he was to do next, when he'd run into the girl. Following her directions, he'd gone to the main house to look for Jackson, and learned he'd just missed him. He'd returned to the barn to see if that's where he'd gone, and heard voices.

Following them, he hadn't realized until it was almost too late that he was overhearing a private conversation between Jackson and his daughter, and that the conversation concerned him.

Mortified, he'd stopped short of walking out the barn doors into the yard, where the pair was seated.

After taking a deep breath, he backtracked down the corridor a bit, then called out, "Jackson?"

"Out here, Tom!"

Biting his lip, Tom hoped the young woman he'd heard begging her father in a quavering voice not to let him come to Ohio had composed herself, and he strolled out through the barn doors as if he'd just discovered where his new employer was hiding. The pretty black Lab woofed once when he appeared, but settled when the young woman reached out and rubbed her silky ears.

Seeing the father and daughter standing awkwardly beside each other, he stopped and looked from one to the other.

He was struck by the remarkable similarities between the two; both tall and red-haired with fiery green eyes and strong builds.

Next, he registered that the daughter, whom he estimated stood just shy of six feet, making her a couple of inches taller than his five-foot-nine-inch height, was dressed like a man, in barn coveralls; the only nod to her gender being the kerchief tied over her pinned-up hair. No wonder he'd momentarily—only momentarily—mistaken her for a man. He darted a glance at her father and wondered uneasily whether he'd been brought in to oust this girl from her preferred occupation on her family's farm. He hoped not, as that would be the type of family drama he could really do without. Especially since he had his own family drama to deal with at the moment.

He ended his reverie, and nodded to the pair. "Um, *guder mariye*. I put my things away in the bunkhouse, and I'm ready to get to work."

"Nonsense! You just got here after a thirty-hour bus ride. You'll have breakfast with the family, and then you'll become familiar with the place. Tomorrow is soon enough to begin learning how we do things around here." Turning to his daughter, with an obvious appeal for peace in his green eyes, Jackson said, "Lida Mae, this is Tom Fisher, all the way from Texas. Maybe you remember him, though he doesn't much resemble the lad you met all those years ago, I suppose."

Lida Mae turned to face her newly arrived nemesis. Summoning a polite, if somewhat stiff smile, she nodded at the young man. "*Ja*, we met a little while ago, when he came in looking for you, *Dat*." She eyeballed him a minute, then shook her head. "It's true, you don't look like I remember. But that was fifteen years ago, and I doubt I look the same, either."

"Well, you're taller than I recall," Tom blurted before closing his eyes in disbelief at his idiocy.

Jackson threw back his head and let out a deep belly laugh. "Oh! That she is, young Tom, that she is. Now, I was just telling Lida Mae that you've come to take over the barn chores and such, so she can get back to doing the woman's work I've kept her from because I needed her help out here."

Tom gave Lida Mae a cautious look, and saw the hurt and anger in her green eyes. Biting his lip, he said nothing, just nodded at Jackson. Was that a little growl he heard her emit?

Turning to her father, Lida Mae narrowed her eyes so he'd know he wasn't off the hook, then spoke sweetly. "I'll go inside and help *Maem* and my sisters get breakfast ready for you menfolk." She flashed a rather toothy and insincere smile at Tom, turned on her booted heel and stomped off around the outside of the barn, followed by the big black dog.

After a few awkward moments, Tom broke the uncomfortable silence. "Um, she seems a bit angry."

"*Ach, ja*, smokin'," Jackson confirmed with a wry nod. "But she'll get over it soon enough. My Lida Mae heats up quick, but she can't hold on to a mad. Not like her mother." He rolled his eyes expressively. "Come on, boy. I'll show you around a bit before breakfast, give her time to cool down."

He stomped off into the dark opening of the barn, and after a moment, Tom slowly followed.

If she was angry that he'd been sent to Ohio to work on a farm he'd never seen with people he didn't know, then she could join the club. It hadn't exactly been his idea to be told in a matter-of-fact way by his *dat* that after careful consideration, he and Tom's *mudder* had decided to leave their property, house, barns and horses to his older brother, Paul. But Tom wasn't to worry, they'd assured him even as he reeled from the blow. Tom and Paul had assumed they would divide the property with their younger brother, Jake. It was plenty big enough for three men to farm, raise horses and families on. But instead of that, Tom was told he was being shipped off to some tiny town in Ohio to learn the ropes of another man's horse ranch, and while he was there, by the way, he should look over the man's three daughters.

That way—and his *dat* had actually winked as he said it—Tom could marry into the property and business nice and neat, and have his own spread since he wouldn't be sharing the one he'd grown up on.

Accustomed to daytime highs in the 60s in winter and the 90s in summer, Tom shuddered at the thought of the ice and snow he'd have to contend with in Ohio.

But he had no intention of staying in Ohio. Jackson's prickly daughter could relax; she was pretty enough, if a person liked tall, outspoken, boyish women who didn't know how a girl was supposed to behave. He preferred small, sweet girls like a certain Amish *maedel* back in Texas. A *maedel* he'd been working up the nerve to ask on a buggy ride when his *dat* had dropped his little bomb about Tom's future.

No, Lida Mae didn't need to worry; while he'd do his job well and learn the routine on her father's horse ranch, he had no intention of wooing Miss Lida Mae Beiler or either of her sisters. Nor did he intend to spend one more day in Ohio, lush and green as it appeared in the summertime, than he had to.

He, Paul and Jake were trying to come up with some way to get him home. He only prayed that they could; once his parents got an idea stuck in their stubborn heads, it was like trying to pry a snapping turtle out of a hole with a straw to convince them to change their minds.

"Coming, Tom?" Jackson called from inside the barn.

"*Ja!* Coming!" he replied, and hurried after his new

boss. For now, he'd need to do his best with what he'd been given—at least until he could think of a way to get back where he belonged. As always, when he felt lost, alone or afraid, he depended on his faith to help him through. He took off his hat, closed his tired eyes and offered up a quick prayer.

Please, Gott, *help me find a way home. For this place is strange, and at least one of the folks here wants me far, far away! Your will be done.*

After a few moments he opened his eyes, plopped his straw hat back onto his tousled hair, and turned to follow Jackson to the house where he now understood he would not receive a universal welcome. He stopped short when he saw Lida Mae blocking his exit, an unhappy look on her face.

"I'm not usually a jerk."

He wasn't sure what to say to that, so he wisely kept his mouth shut and waited to see what else she had to say.

She scuffed the floor with her booted foot, and huffed out a sigh. "I guess you overheard most of what I said to my *daed*?"

He shrugged, embarrassed. "Sorry about that."

"Well, there's nothing to be done about it now." She narrowed a look at him. "Tom, I don't know why you came here to steal my life, but understand this. I don't want you here, and while I won't go against my parents' wishes, I'm not going to go out of my way to make your life easier. And I have absolutely no interest in marrying you, so don't even bother to go down that road!"

With that, she turned and left Tom standing alone, mouth agape, staring after her. "I didn't ask you to marry me," he said to no one.

He'd thought she was out of earshot, but an answering

shout of, "Good!" echoed back to him from somewhere down the long corridor.

"Ach. This is not a *gut* start." Pushing his hat more firmly onto his head, he followed his fiery nemesis out of the barn, hoping they could get through supper without any more unpleasantness.

Chapter Two

Lida Mae ambled along the sidewalk in downtown Charm, letting the stick in her hand clatter along the pickets of a wooden fence in front of a big, green house. She'd just run to the post office and was poking along on her way back, brooding about her situation.

She was staring at her feet as she walked, which was why she didn't see her sisters, Rhoda and Priscilla, approaching until four sneakers, two blue and two white, entered her field of vision. She looked up sharply into the smirking faces of her older sisters.

"Hello, Lida Mae," Rhoda, cheerfully greeted her. "Are you watching to be sure you don't step on any cracks? *Maem* will be grateful you're thoughtfully protecting her back."

Priscilla shook her head. "Silly," she said to Rhoda. "She's obviously testing the fence for musicality. I think it sounds a little wooden, personally."

Lida Mae rolled her eyes. "Stop trying to cheer me up. I'm determined to stay angry at *Dat* and *Maem*. They're ruining my life."

She tossed away the stick and commenced walking. Priscilla and Rhoda exchanged uneasy looks, then fell in on either side of Lida Mae. "Staying angry at our parents is a sin, Lida Mae. You need to give this to *Gott*, and try to accept the way things are now," Priscilla suggested in an attempt at big-sister wisdom.

Rhoda nodded emphatically. "*Ja*, Prissy is right. It's not as if being mad will change anything. It'll just give you indigestion and permanent frown lines. You're much too young and lovely for that!"

Lida Mae snorted and kept walking, her long strides forcing her much shorter sisters to hustle to keep up. Young she might be at twenty, but lovely? Apparently not by the standards of her Amish church community. Otherwise, why hadn't a single man offered to take her for a buggy ride after a gathering? Why hadn't any of the boys she knew come to sit on the porch swing in the evening, just to chat and drink lemonade? She knew the problem was her height. She towered over all the women and most of the men in her district. Her mother kept telling her it didn't matter, but having observed both Priscilla and Rhoda fending off scads of boys attracted by their dainty femininity, she was having trouble believing it.

Rhoda slapped her lightly on the arm. "*Ach!* Slow down! I'm getting a stitch."

When Lida Mae grudgingly shortened her strides, her sisters breathed twin sighs of relief. "I know what you're thinking, Lida Mae," Rhoda panted. "You're thinking you're too tall to be considered attractive. But we keep telling you, that's not *your* problem. The problem is the men around here. Look at you! You have gorgeous red hair, the color of a new penny. Your skin is flawless, except for that darling dusting of freckles across the bridge of your nose. And your eyes are like fresh spring grass. Just like *Dat's*! You're beautiful, that's what you are."

Priscilla nodded. "*Ja.* You are. It's too bad the men around here are so *dumm*."

"*Ja.* After all, you look just like *Dat*, and he's widely regarded as being a handsome man, right?" Rhoda pointed out reasonably.

Lida Mae pursed her lips. "It's different for men. And, anyway, we're not supposed to be all about outer appearances, are we? But everyone is. Hypocrites. I'm tired of it. While I was working on the farm and thought I'd inherit the business someday, I could convince myself it didn't matter if no man ever wanted me. I'd be an independent woman. If I never married and had *kinner*, I could spoil yours. But now that *Dat* and *Maem* have taken that away from me and want me to behave like a *proper lady*, what am I supposed to do? They're trying to make me into something I'm not, and it's just not going to work!" Her eyes flooded with tears.

"Oh, Lida Mae, don't cry. You'll see, it'll all work out." Priscilla wrapped an arm around her younger sister's waist—she couldn't reach her shoulders, since Lida Mae stood a good ten inches taller.

Lida Mae stopped and spun to face both sisters, nearly tipping Priscilla over onto her *hinnerdale*. "Do you know what *Dat* said to me? Do you?" They both stared at her mutely and shook their heads.

Lida Mae sniffed and wiped her nose on the back of her sleeve. She nodded absently when Rhoda handed her a tissue. "He said I was *pretty enough, if a bit tall*—that all I needed was a bit of polishing... Polishing! And I'd attract a man in no time." She sniffled loudly. "Can you believe it? My own *dat*!"

Priscilla and Rhoda bit their lips and looked miserable.

"You have to admit, he made her sound like a horse," Rhoda murmured.

"Well, *Dat* isn't exactly diplomatic," Priscilla offered. "Remember when Aunt Lucy had chicken pox in her forties? She was worried she'd get scars, and *Dat* said she was already married, and too old to care about how she looked."

Lida Mae snorted out a teary giggle despite herself. "*Maem* had to do some fast talking to make Aunt Lucy feel better. And she's *Dat's* sister!"

"*Ja*, so don't pay attention to what he says. The right man will come along, and he'll see *you*. Not your height. Not your clothes. You." Rhoda offered her sister an encouraging smile.

Lida Mae cast a wry glance at her sister, and one corner of her mouth tilted up. "You might take your own advice, sister mine."

Rhoda blew a raspberry and rolled her eyes. "I'm done with men. We're talking about you."

"Not anymore, we aren't. Thanks for trying to cheer me up." She impulsively hugged first Rhoda, and then Priscilla, then drew back to look earnestly at her older siblings. "But, guys, if you really want to help, you could help me find a way to get rid of that Fisher boy, and reclaim my place in the family horse business!"

When they just stared at her, mouths agape, she snorted. "You look like fish."

"But, Lida Mae, you're asking us to go against *Maem's* and *Dat's* wishes. We can't do that. It wouldn't be right. You have to trust them, even though I admit I can't exactly see where their plan is going at the moment," Priscilla said.

Rhoda gave her older sister the side-eye, then turned

to Lida Mae. "While I don't totally agree with Priscilla, I do have to say that *Maem* and *Dat* have the right to decide who will work on the farm." When Lida Mae opened her mouth to protest, Rhoda raised a hand. "I didn't say they're right to try to force you to become just like us. You're fine the way you are. But I agree we can't openly go against their wishes."

Lida Mae cast her eyes down in dejection, and Rhoda stepped in and hugged her. "I didn't say I wouldn't help. Just that I won't openly go against them, *fashtay*?"

Lida Mae regarded her sister hopefully and nodded. "*Ja*, I understand. So…you will help, but you don't want to get caught, ain't so?"

Rhoda laughed and nodded. "That about sums it up. If it makes me a coward, I'm sorry." Then she looked at Priscilla. "Are you in, Prissy?"

When Priscilla hesitated, Rhoda narrowed her eyes. "At least agree not to tell *Maem* and *Dat* that we're trying to figure out a way to get Lida Mae back to farming."

Priscilla heaved a sigh and nodded slowly. "*Ja*, I can agree to that. Give me time to think about the rest. I see no reason why Lida Mae shouldn't be able to farm—lots of women do. But we can't go against *Maem* and *Dat*. We have to find a way around that."

"A sneaky way," Rhoda murmured.

Priscilla's lips quirked, but she didn't quite smile. "A respectful way."

They all looked at each other and nodded. *"Denki,"* Lida Mae said. "I feel a bit better, truly." She started walking again, her sisters falling in beside her.

"Don't thank us yet. Tom Fisher still has your job, and unless you marry him to get it back, I don't see how we're going to get around this," Priscilla said.

Lida Mae stopped in her tracks and looked at her sisters, who had to turn to face her as they'd kept going for a few steps. "Marry Tom! Not if he was the last man in Ohio!"

Suddenly, Priscilla's and Rhoda's eyes widened in alarm, but before Lida Mae could turn around to see what was behind her, a deep voice declared, "I don't recall asking you."

Closing her eyes, Lida Mae sent up a prayer that when she turned around, Tom Fisher wouldn't be standing there, having overheard her unfortunate remark. She threw her sisters panicked looks, but they just shook their heads and shrugged helplessly. Lida Mae steeled herself and turned slowly around, just as Priscilla jumped into the conversational breach.

"Why, Tom! Where did you come from? We were just…discussing, um, family matters," Priscilla said in a falsely cheerful tone of voice.

Lida Mae cast her sister a disbelieving look, sighed and turned her eyes to Tom, who was standing hipshot, one hand shoved into the pocket of his barn jacket and the other holding a bag from the hardware store. His straw hat somehow managed to look natty as it covered his black hair. His brown eyes were narrowed to slits as he glared at Lida Mae.

"Um, hi, Tom. What's up?" Lida Mae asked him lamely.

"I heard what you were discussing. And don't worry, Lida Mae, I wouldn't marry you if you were the last girl in Texas! It just so happens there's a girl back home waiting for me. So you can relax. I'm not after your hand, or your farm." He looked at the bag he was carrying, and thrust it into Lida Mae's hands. "Here. Your *dat* asked me to bring this down to your mother at the quilt shop. Consider it delivered. Now, if you'll excuse me, I've got to get back to doing the job you want, but can't have, and that I don't want, and have no choice but to do!"

He turned and stalked off down the sidewalk, leaving the three sisters staring, open-mouthed, at his stiffly retreating back.

Finally, Rhoda cleared her throat. "Well, that was awkward."

"Pretty awkward, *ja*," Priscilla agreed.

Lida Mae threw up her hands, nearly braining Rhoda with the bag Tom had given her to deliver to their *maem*. "Oh! I can't believe he heard that! He's going to think I've set my cap for him. Could things get any worse? I didn't think they could before, but I was obviously wrong!"

"Actually, based on what he heard you say, he'd think the opposite, right?" Rhoda called after her sister. "Besides, he said he has a girlfriend, so Prissy's suggestion wouldn't work anyway!"

"*Ach!* I don't know when I've ever been more embarrassed!" Lida Mae hurried toward the quilt shop, and her sisters scurried after her.

"Lida Mae! Wait up!" Rhoda called, but she didn't slow her pace.

"Oh, come on, give us a break," Priscilla gasped, nearly running to catch up to Lida Mae, who suddenly swerved around to face her sisters, hands on her hips.

She poked Priscilla in the chest, and her sister raised a hand to rub at the spot. "Ow!"

"Serves you right! If you hadn't said that about me marrying Tom to get the farm back, I wouldn't have said what I did, and he wouldn't think I've set my cap for him! I'm so mad I could spit!"

"Please don't," Rhoda said, then cringed at Lida Mae's furious glare. "Er, I mean, it's unhygienic."

"You know, maybe you shouldn't give up on marrying Tom so easily," Priscilla said. "His so-called girlfriend is pretty far away, and it occurs to me that you wouldn't be so concerned about what he thinks about you if you weren't at least a little bit attracted to him. Hmmm?"

"Oh!" Lida Mae turned toward the shop again. "You're both hopeless! Just leave me alone. I have to figure out what to do now. I can't face that—that…interloper again today! I may have to sleep at the shop!"

Lida Mae stalked up the steps and entered Beiler's Amish Quilts feeling about as bad as she had the previous week, when her parents had delivered what Lida Mae was privately coming to think of as The Crushing Blow. She just needed to be alone for a little while. She had to remember that her sisters had promised they would help her find a way around this dilemma. "And marrying Tom Fisher is definitely not on the agenda," she sputtered. "Whether he has a girlfriend back in Texas or not."

"What's that, dear?" Her mother's question had Lida Mae looking up, and she groaned when she saw that the pair of *Englisch* women who had been dithering over several baby quilts when she'd left for the post office were still there. She pasted a fake smile on her face and hoped it would fool the tourists; her *maem* would see right through it. Her sisters crowded in through the door behind her, nearly running into her, and she moved forward.

In a conscious attempt to appear normal—whatever that was—she smiled at her mother. "Nothing, *Maem*. You got a letter from Aunt Kitty." She carried the mail up to the counter, where her mother stood helping their customers. She noticed they'd decided on a sweet blue-

and-white crib quilt with a pattern of little bunnies hopping around on a background of cabbages and carrots. It was one she'd made, and really liked. She was glad it was going to a new home, and that feeling softened her angst and anger a bit. "Nice choice," she said, and smiled at the women, who smiled back.

"*Maem*, I'll be in the back, working on the quilt on the frame. It's due to be finished by the weekend. Call me if you need me." With a last nod at the customers, she turned and made her way to the back of the shop, and a little sister-free peace and quiet.

Tom frowned fiercely as he hung up the phone in the Beilers's barn. He leaned back in the hard wooden chair at Jackson's desk, and repeatedly pulled on his lower lip while he pondered what his brother Jake had just told him.

A year younger than Tom, Jake, who had lost an arm in a childhood accident, had just confided in Tom that he had no idea what he was going to do, because as many ways as he and their oldest brother, Paul, tried to approach their father about all of them wanting to share the land and work together, their stubborn *dat* wouldn't be budged.

"He's gotten it in his head that this is the way it should be, and that's that," Tom muttered. "I'm not ready to give up yet, but I'd better start considering that there really may not be a place for me back home anymore."

As maddening as the situation was, he and his brothers had been firmly raised to respect and not question their parents' judgment, which made the current situation more difficult.

What if they're right? What if this is where I'm supposed to be?

He drummed his fingers on the old wood desk, and

puzzled over what Jake had said. It seemed that even their *maem* had tried reasoning with *Dat*, but he'd told her that while he appreciated her concern for her boys, she should trust him, and all would come out fine.

"How does he figure that? I'm unhappy here, and Jake has nowhere to go! He's used to the way we do things on the home place. How is he going to adapt to someone else's spread? Somewhere they'll undoubtedly expect their hired hands to have two hands!"

Jake had thrown another wrench into the works of Tom's plans to return home when he mentioned, a little bit too casually as if trying to sound like he didn't know it would be a big deal, that the girl Tom liked back home—the one he'd claimed was his girlfriend earlier that day—had recently gotten engaged to a young man from an Amish community in Wisconsin.

Tom dropped his face into his hands, rubbing at his sore temples. "Oh, *sis yuscht*. So much for that. Not that she gave me any indication that she'd wait for me, but still, I kind of hoped she would."

And then there was the unexpected confrontation with Lida Mae earlier that day. "Why did she make me so angry? I behaved like a *boppli*. But why would she say such a mean thing, anyway? This whole situation just keeps getting worse and worse."

Tom climbed to his feet and headed for the buggy barn. He'd noticed earlier that the tack for the buggy horses needed to be cleaned and conditioned, and his father had taught him and his *brudders* that proper care of equipment was part of proper care of the horses.

He could still hear his father preaching: "It's not all about galloping around on horses and having fun, boys. Farming and ranching are hard work!"

Since he hadn't been assigned any particular chores that morning, he figured that the necessary, if tedious, chore of cleaning and conditioning tack was as good a place to start as any.

Jackson found him sitting on a bench in the buggy barn about an hour later, one set of tack taken apart and sitting around him in various stages of being cleaned and conditioned. Tom glanced up from rubbing saddle soap off a bridle and nodded at his boss, who quirked a bushy red eyebrow his way.

"You look mighty industrious there, Tom. *Denki*—I've been meaning to get to that. It's usually Lida Mae's job, but..." The older man let his sentence drop, looking uncomfortable, and Tom simply waited to see if he would finish what he'd started to say.

When he didn't, Tom decided to pry just a little, in hopes he could learn why the infuriating girl still wouldn't give him the time of day.

"So Lida Mae usually cleans the tack?"

Jackson shot him a guilty look, and shrugged. "Well, it was her job before, *ja*. But not anymore."

"She decided she didn't like cleaning tack?" Tom persisted.

"I suppose she liked it fine."

It's like prying open an oyster, getting the man to talk.

"Oh, then maybe I shouldn't do it. I wouldn't want her to think I was trying to take over her duties or anything. To tell you the truth, Jackson, she's seemed kind of sore at me since I arrived."

Jackson folded his arms and pursed his lips as if considering what to say. Then he heaved a huge sigh, and nodded. "*Ja*, she's sore, but not really at you. More at her *maem* and me. You see, before you got here, she was pretty much my right-hand man. Er, *maedel*. Anyway, she took care of things like keeping all the leather clean and conditioned, and keeping the hardware in good shape. She exercised a lot of the horses, mucked the stalls, fed and groomed. And she was shaping up to be a pretty good trainer, too." He frowned. "Plus, I noticed a few years ago she's got a really good eye for which mares will pair best with which studs to produce the nicest foals."

Tom frowned. *Why would Jackson and Clara stop their clearly competent daughter from doing the chores she loved doing? Do they really even need me here?*

He cleared his throat. "So, if Lida Mae is that *gut* at farm chores, why not let her do them?"

Jackson sighed again. "Her *mudder* decided that at twenty Lida Mae was wasting her time hanging out with her old man all day, dressing like a boy. And she was right. So I called your *dat*, and arranged for you to come take Lida Mae's place. And here you are."

Tom's mouth fell open at this last part of Jackson's explanation. The polishing cloth hung, forgotten, from his hand. He blinked. "Wait. So you're saying that pretty much all her life your daughter has worked the farm and horses with you?"

Jackson nodded, looking both stubborn and miserable, and Tom inwardly cringed. *This is why the maedel can't stand me! I've invaded her territory and displaced her. I see now why she accused me of stealing her life. I basically did!* Striving for calm, he continued. "You have no sons, right? So if Lida Mae worked with you all these years, did she expect to inherit the whole operation from you someday?" He bit his lip, waiting for Jackson's answer; but he already knew what it would be.

Jackson turned a miserable look on the younger man

and nodded. "*Ja.* I guess I didn't realize that's what she was thinking until the day you came. I guess I misled her all these years. When I told her she wouldn't have to work on the farm anymore, she told me she'd expected to inherit and continue the business. She told me it was her dream."

He shook his head, and ran a big, work-roughened hand through his red hair. "But how could that be? Lida Mae is a woman. And farmwork, horse breaking, all of it is man's work."

Tom stared at Jackson for a few seconds, then cleared his throat. "Well, where I come from, plenty of women work their ranches right alongside their men."

"*Englisch* women, sure," Jackson said, picking up a piece of straw from the floor of the barn and twisting it between his fingers.

"Amish women, too," Tom said. "We grow them tough and strong in Texas. I guess maybe Lida Mae isn't strong enough for the work, huh?"

Jackson glared at Tom. "Now, hold on. Lida Mae is as tough as they come. And strong, too. You should see her handle a feisty horse."

Tom waited a minute, then ventured, "Then why did you decide to make her stop doing it?"

Jackson stared at the straw in his hand. "Her *mudder*. She never did like that Lida Mae worked out here with me. The other girls are small and dainty, like my Clara. But as you've seen, Lida Mae is tall and strong like me." He smiled a moment, then shook his head. "But the house is her mother's domain, and she wanted her baby girl back in it and out of the barn. And that was that." He looked pointedly at Tom. "Don't think to change anything about that, young Tom. Not to be rude, but it ain't your business. Lida Mae will do fine learning how to be a *fraa* and *mudder.* You're doing fine working here with me. And that's how it's got to stay."

He pushed to his feet. "Well, it's about lunchtime. Why don't you finish that job after we eat? Clara and the girls are at the shop, but I expect she's left us a *gut* meal in the oven." He stopped and turned to look at Tom. "I'd appreciate it if you didn't repeat any of what I told you, Tom. I really shouldn't have said all I did. But while you're a fine worker, and I'm blessed to have you here, I do miss working with that girl. She has a way of making you laugh."

No sign of laughter on his face, Jackson turned and left the barn. Tom stared after him, realizing that he wasn't the only one whose expectations had been dashed. Sure, he'd realized she hadn't wanted him here; even suspected she was hoping to inherit the spread. But he hadn't known how long she'd spent nurturing that dream, encouraged by her father every bit as much as he and his *brudders* had been encouraged by their *dat* to believe things were going to be a certain way…only to pull the rug out from under their feet and let them fall where they would.

He and Lida Mae hadn't been given any more say in their own futures than any of the horses they raised on their ranches got.

"It's not right, but there's not a thing I can do about it," he whispered as he put down the tools and prepared to head in to lunch. "I can't even solve my own problem."

He had a new sympathy for the young woman who couldn't look at him without scowling, and wouldn't marry him if he was the last boy in Ohio. At least he now understood why.

It was bad enough being sent away from his family ranch. What if instead, he'd been told he was going to have to sit by and watch some stranger come in and work with his father, helpless to stop it?

"*Ja*, I understand why she glares at me so much. I wish there were a way to fix this situation for both of us."

He walked to the house, and was greeted by Lida Mae and Rhoda's dogs. Giving them each some ear rubs, he sent up a silent prayer.

Father, please help me either to accept or change my situation. Help Lida Mae, too. Everything is such a mess! And all because our parents have gotten these ideas into their heads and we're powerless to change their minds. And please help Jake and Paul, too. I'm trying to do a gut job, but I'm not happy, Father. And... Lida Mae may be thorny as a prickly pear cactus, but she doesn't deserve this! But, in this, as in all things, Your will be done, Father.

Standing outside the house, hands on his hips, he pondered the similarities between his younger *brudder* Jake's and Lida Mae's predicaments. Jake had lost an arm, but he'd figured out many ways to work around the disability, and was as good a rancher as any man Tom knew. But not everyone saw it that way, which was why Jake was still looking for a position of his own back in Texas.

The prejudice Jake is experiencing due to his missing arm isn't really all that different from Lida Mae having to give up what she loves because she's a woman rather than a man. Jackson is right; while some Amish wives work alongside their husbands on farms and ranches, it's not as common as it is in the Englischer *world. But if Lida Mae were my* fraa, *I'd be grateful for her strength and skill! I'd be proud to have her working beside me!*

Tom caught the direction of his thoughts and gave a hard mental tug on his reins. "Whoa, boy. Where did that come from? You're no more interested in her that way than she is in you! Better concentrate on figuring out how you can get back home where you belong and forget Lida Mae and her red-head's temper! You've got enough problems without taking on a cactus of a wife."

He took a deep, cleansing breath before heading into the kitchen. With *Gott's* help, he fully believed that everything would, eventually, come out right. Eventually. He just had to figure out what he was supposed to do to make that happen. Sit back and go with the flow, or swim upstream against the current? Either way meant trouble, for sure and certain!

But maybe if he put his mind to it, he could come up with a way to help Lida Mae. How, he wasn't sure. And she certainly wouldn't appreciate him meddling in her life. But if he couldn't help himself and his *brudders*, at least he'd be helping someone.

Chapter Three

After first making sure that Tom was occupied with her father working with a young colt on a lunge line in the outdoor ring, Lida Mae and Blue walked up the stone path to what the family called the bunkhouse. In truth, it was a two-story cottage with four bedrooms occasionally used by visiting hands, such as Tom, at the moment.

The little house had one full-time occupant, who was the reason for Lida Mae's visit on this fine, early summer day. As she'd hoped, old Obadiah was sitting in his rocking chair on the covered porch, soaking in some late-morning rays, his ancient Labrador, Ethel, curled up in a patch of sunshine near his feet.

"Guder mariye, Obadiah!" At her call, Ethel raised her head and opened her eyes. Seeing Lida Mae and Blue, she gave a little woof of welcome and went back to her nap.

Blue, who was Ethel's granddaughter, whined for permission to go join the elderly dog, and Lida Mae patted her on the head and told her to go visit. The young dog trotted up on the porch, tongue lolling happily from her mouth, first greeting Obadiah, who scratched her under her whiskery chin, and then headed over to curl up in the sun next to her grandmother. The doggie matriarch nuzzled Blue, then went back to sleep. Her granddaughter lay in the sun, keeping an eye on her mistress.

Obadiah gestured for Lida Mae to take the other rocking chair and chuckled at her dog's antics. "That girl of yours isn't going to take her eyes off you the whole time you're here. She's a *gut* one, that. Just like her *maem* and her *grossmammi* before her."

Lida Mae smiled at her dog and nodded. "*Ja*, I don't know how I got along before I had her."

Obadiah nodded, then cast a sideways glance at Lida Mae, who was still smiling at the dogs. "Well, I doubt you came here to talk to an old man about dogs. If I had to guess, I'd suppose you're here to discuss a certain young man who arrived recently, and the impact that young man's arrival has had on your own routine."

"You do know me well." She raised troubled, impatient green eyes to calmer, faded blue ones. "My *schwestern* think I should leave it alone and honor *Maem* and *Dat's* will. But, Obadiah, I'm not cut out to be a traditional Amish wife." She practically wailed the last bit.

The old man, who was like a grandfather to Lida Mae and her sisters, took a slow sip of the *kaffi* that was sitting on the table next to him and thought about it for a minute or two before speaking. She knew better than to interrupt. Finally, he let out a *harrumph* and turned to study the oats growing in a field off to the east. "Well, since you ask, Lida Mae, I'll tell you that, while I disagree with your folks about this, I'd have to remind you that we are to honor our parents. It's *Gott's* will, *nee*?"

Lida Mae gave an unhappy nod.

"Then I'm not sure why you're asking me. You already know the answer. I'd say give it time. It won't hurt you to get better at womanly arts. And the boy's not so bad.

Give him a chance, why don't you? You might find you have a lot in common."

When Lida Mae opened her mouth to give a heated reply, Obadiah held up a hand grown twisted with arthritis. "Now, hold on, girl. Don't get all in a tither! You know I'm right about learning women's arts and such. It never hurts to become better at anything." He waited for her to give a reluctant nod of agreement, and huffed at her. "That don't mean I think you should give up farmwork permanently. I think after a while, your *dat* and *maem* will realize it don't need to be all or nothin'." He gave a sage nod. "Then they'll let you get back to what you love. But you have to be patient, which I don't mind reminding you is not your strong suit."

He took another sip of *kaffi*, then thumped the empty mug back down on the table. "Any more questions? Or can an old man go inside and get his lunch?"

"Aren't you eating at the main house today?"

"*Nee*, my arthritis is acting up a bit. That old woman from down the road is supposed to come by with some of her herbal remedies, and I don't want to miss her. You go on."

Lida Mae knew Obadiah referred to their neighbor from down the lane, Rebekah Schwartz, who was an herbal healer much respected in their part of Ohio. She sold her remedies online with the help of a granddaughter who had a shop and computer in town. But for old Obadiah, whom Lida Mae suspected she was sweet on, she made house calls. And Lida Mae didn't think the old woman's partiality was one-sided.

I wonder why he doesn't just ask her to marry him? Rebekah has plenty of room in her little house, and I think they'd suit each other very well. But I'm no match-

maker, so I'll mind my own business, or I'll be getting another lecture.

"Okay, thanks for the advice." She pushed to her feet and Blue jumped to hers. "I'll see you later. Need anything from the house, or from town?"

"*Nee, nee.* Come by more often, though. You don't need a reason."

Lida Mae couldn't resist teasing Obadiah a tiny bit. "Enjoy your visit with Rebekah. I think she liiikes you!"

At his cranky, mumbled response, Lida Mae laughed delightedly and leaned down to give the old man a kiss on his whiskered cheek. When Blue gave two sharp woofs, she looked around to see Tom standing on the path leading up to the cottage.

"Tom!" She shifted awkwardly. "Um, I didn't expect to run into you. I came to see Obadiah and Ethel."

Behind her, Obadiah gave a cackle, and Lida Mae shot him a pleading glance and prayed he didn't decide to take a little revenge on her for the remark about Rebekah. "She's telling the truth, Tom. Just stopped by to pass the time of day with an old man." She turned sheepishly back to Tom, who was regarding her in a knowing—and oddly sympathetic—way. *What's that about?* "Er, I'm just heading up to the house for lunch. I won't keep you." She skipped down the porch steps, and skirted past Tom on her way to the main house, careful not to touch him. She'd just breathed a sigh of relief at having avoided a conversation, when he called after her.

"Wait up a minute, Lida Mae. I just want to wash my hands, and I'll walk with you to lunch."

She sucked in a breath and rolled her eyes, her back to him. "You don't have to do that. I know the way."

She heard a chuckle and turned to see Obadiah sitting alone on the porch. Tom must have gone in to wash his hands. She glared at her old friend. "What are you laughing at?"

He took off his straw hat and wiped his brow with a handkerchief before shaking his grizzled, gray head, his long beard waving a bit in a breeze as he tried to look innocent. "Me? Nothing at all. I'm just amused at youth. *Gut* thing you're young, I say, because you waste so much time fighting against the inevitable. We old folks know we don't have that time to waste. And we don't need young'uns reminding us of the fact." He looked past her and his face became wreathed in a big, welcoming smile. Lida Mae turned and grinned at Rebekah, who was making her slow way toward them from the driveway, where Lida Mae could see her pony and cart tethered to a hitching rail. A pretty basket was looped over the healer's arm.

"Hello, Rebekah. *Wie bischt?*"

"Fine, fine, Lida Mae." She fanned her face a bit and grimaced. "Though it is mighty warm today, I declare! I can barely catch my breath!" She bent and rubbed between Blue's ears. "And here's my *gut* girl, Blue!"

Lida Mae heard hurried steps, and turned to see Tom reappear. Feeling an odd, squirmy sensation in her belly at his approach, she drew a breath, wondering why she was reacting this way. No other man had ever had the effect on her that this interloper did, making her feel as if her stomach were full of butterflies, or maybe eels. Praying her discomfort didn't show on her face, and that Tom couldn't tell how she felt, she forced a smile and introduced him to the healer. "Rebekah, this is our new hand, Tom Fisher, from Texas. Tom, this is our local herbal healer, Rebekah Schwartz."

Brown eyes bright with interest, Tom shook the old

lady's hand. "*Guder mariye.* We have an herbal healer back home we all think very highly of."

"That's *gut* to hear. What brings you here, Tom?"

Tom cast a nervous glance at Lida Mae, as if worried that she would take the opportunity to air their differences. She rolled her eyes. While she'd like to say a few choice things to him, she wouldn't do it in front of her elders. She only folded her arms and stared back, and, apparently relieved that she'd decided not to let the older woman know how she felt about him, Tom said, "Er, my family has a horse ranch near Beeville, and *Dat* thought it would be *gut* for me to learn some different ways."

Unable to help herself, Lida Mae snorted, drawing a frown from Tom. Before he could comment, she turned to Rebekah and said, "Yes, we're so glad Tom is here to help *Dat* with all the men's work on the farm. But now we need to get in to lunch. Don't let Obadiah convince you his hands and feet aren't hurting something fierce!"

At the old man's protest, Lida Mae sent him a sweet smile. "I've seen you limping, Obadiah. And you won't use a cane. So be honest with Rebekah." With that, she nodded at Rebekah and, ignoring Tom, turned to walk to the house. Tom fell into step beside her, hands thrust into his pockets. He glanced at her—she could feel it—but he didn't speak.

I might as well take this opportunity to tell him what I think, while nobody can hear. She stopped walking, and glanced back to see Obadiah and Rebekah engaged in conversation. "They won't notice us. Come on." She grabbed his hand and pulled him around to the side of the house, away from the kitchen where her *dat* was probably waiting for them to eat.

"Hey, what are you doing?" Tom grumbled as she released his hand and turned to face him.

"We need to talk."

He nodded slowly. "*Ja*, we do. Actually, that's why I asked you to wait for me while I washed my hands. But then we got all turned around and I forgot."

"You wanted to talk to me? Why?" She suddenly recalled the odd, sympathetic look on his face when he'd found her at the bunk house, and suspicion bloomed in her chest.

"Did my *dat* say something to you about me?"

Tom looked startled, and then he cast his eyes to the ground, avoiding her. "Um, like what?"

Now she knew her *dat* had blabbed to Tom about her! Probably told him she couldn't hold up her end of the farm and ranch work, and how glad he was to have a man arrive to take over her chores!

She was furious when she felt the sting of tears in her eyes, and rubbed at one as if she'd gotten a speck in it.

"Oh, *sis yuscht*! Don't cry!"

Okay, she hadn't fooled him. And that only made her madder. "Why did you want to talk to me, anyway?"

He looked lost for a moment, as if he couldn't recall. "Well, maybe your *dat* did mention that you weren't happy to have me here because I'd been brought here to take your place working around the farm." At her angry hiss, he held up a placating hand. "Lida Mae, give me a break, please. I didn't ask to come here, and I don't want to take over your life, as you said. I've got my own perfectly *gut* life back in Texas! Believe me, I'd rather be there, and my brothers and I are doing everything we can to get me back home."

"Right, because you have a girlfriend there who's not the last girl you'd ever marry."

"As to that, I found out today that she just got engaged to someone else. So that's off the table."

Lida Mae's mouth formed a little "o" of surprise. "*Ach,* I'm sorry, Tom. That stinks."

He gave an uncomfortable shrug. "We weren't exactly courting anyway. I may have exaggerated that a little bit. So it's no big deal."

"Oh. Still, it's hard. So, sorry."

"Thanks, I guess." He looked at her, uncertainty in his gaze. "Look, can we call a truce? Maybe if we work together instead of bickering all the time, we can figure out a way to make both of us happy."

She narrowed her eyes at him, unsure she could trust his sudden about face. Sure, he was coming off all reasonable at the moment, but did she really know this guy? What if he was playing her? What did she know about him?

She took a step closer to him, lowering her voice. "Okay, if you're in such a hurry to get home, tell me why. Why would a handsome guy like you with a big ranch that makes Beiler Horses look puny come to Ohio if not to find a wife and horn in on her family ranch and on her life? Hmmm? Can you tell me that?"

She waited smugly for him to crumble under her interrogation and confess his true motives, but at that moment the kitchen window flew open and her sister Rhoda, whom she'd thought was in town at the quilt shop, leaned out.

"There you two are! Come on, lunch is about ready and we could use some help!"

"Coming, Rhoda," Lida Mae said. She turned back to

Tom, who was looking at her as if he hadn't heard her correctly.

"I have no idea where you got those notions, but I can promise you you're mistaken," he began, but she held up a hand to stop him.

"We're out of time. Just know this, Tom Fisher; I'm watching you, and I'm not going to fall for any of your charming cowboy lines, got it? We'll talk again, but for now, please just try to stay out of my way, *fashtay*?"

He shrugged, his face blanking. "Sure, I understand. Later." He turned, and she suddenly remembered he'd said he wanted to talk.

"Wait!" He paused, but didn't look back at her. She swallowed a feeling that maybe she was somehow the one in the wrong. "What did you want to talk to me about?"

He turned and gave her a scathing glance. "How on earth would I remember after the way you just spoke to me? I'll see you inside." He walked off, leaving her feeling certain that she'd been too hard on him. But she'd seen red there for a moment—one of her failings. She sometimes couldn't control her temper. Her *maem* was always after her about it.

Reluctantly, she followed Tom into the house, hoping she hadn't made a fool of herself, but still unable to bring herself to trust him, even if he was ridiculously handsome, and even if he did make her insides feel all squishy. She did wonder what he wanted to discuss with her, though.

I'll be polite as can be the next chance we get to talk. That should make up for my recent bout of crabbiness, which only happened because I was embarrassed that Tom saw me cry. Oh, sis yuscht*!*

Inside, they found Clara and Rhoda setting the table.

"*Maem*, Rhoda, you're back early," Lida Mae commented as she headed to the sink to wash her hands.

"I have a bit of a headache, dear, so I thought I'd come home for lunch and maybe take a little nap afterward. Rhoda is headed back to the shop after we eat."

"Oh, that works," Lida Mae said to Rhoda. "I'll ride back with you after lunch, and Priscilla can head home."

Clara looked from Lida Mae to Tom, who was standing quietly just inside the door. "You two are a bit early, but you can help get the table ready."

They did, moving around each other carefully so as not to risk accidentally touching.

When the table was set, Rhoda stepped out onto the porch and rang the large dinner triangle with the iron striker hanging next to it on the wall of the house.

"Okay!" Jackson said as he entered. "Let's eat. I'm starving!" After taking their seats, they bent their heads for the silent mealtime prayer, and soon they were all reaching around to help themselves to the *gut* lunch Clara and Rhoda had prepared, passing dishes and chattering with each other.

Lida Mae noticed how easily Tom seemed to fit in with her family. She realized she was the only one who seemed to have a problem with him; a thought that made her feel small and churlish.

"Everything okay, Lida Mae?" Rhoda's soft whisper pulled her from her dark thoughts, and she realized she was holding a chicken drumstick fiercely in her hand, glaring at her plate. "Oh, *ja. Denki.* Got lost in my thoughts."

Rhoda smirked. "I could tell. And so will everyone else if you don't chill, sis."

Lida Mae schooled her features and took a determined

bite of the excellent fried chicken. "*Ach*, this is so *gut*, *Maem*!"

"I made that, *denki*," Rhoda said with another smirk. Lida Mae grinned unrepentantly at her older sister and tucked into her meal. Just because she was grumpy didn't mean she had to go hungry. What would be the point in that?

Tom reached for a second drumstick, filling his mouth so he wouldn't be expected to participate in the lunchtime conversation. Rhoda and Lida Mae were murmuring quietly to one another, and Jackson and Clara were busily filling each other in on their respective mornings.

Tom swallowed a sudden lump of loneliness that threatened to keep the chicken from finding its way to his stomach. He missed his own parents and brothers, and their lively mealtime conversations. He reached for his glass of milk to wash it down, wondering whether he'd ever be really happy again, when suddenly the dogs started barking loudly, almost covering up the faint cries for help he could hear coming from outside.

"What's that?" Jackson jumped up, followed by Tom. They rushed to the door, the women close behind, to see Obadiah crouched over the prone figure of Rebekah, who was lying motionless on the bunkhouse porch.

Clara's hands flew to her mouth. "Rebekah's ill! Rhoda, run to the barn and call nine-one-one!"

Tom raced across the yard, knowing he might not have much time, and hoping the old woman wasn't already beyond human help. Obadiah raised a teary face to Tom as he jumped up onto the porch. "Tom! Something's wrong with Rebekah! I don't know what to do! Help her, please!"

Tom knew he didn't have time to comfort the old man.

He kneeled beside Rebekah and felt for a pulse in her throat. He gasped when he found one, faint and thready. It stuttered to a halt even as he registered its existence. But Tom had felt it, so he had to believe it wasn't too late. "She's alive yet, Tom! Pray! Let me in closer. I need room so I can help her."

Clara and Jackson had arrived, and helped Obadiah stand up and move back into his chair. Lida Mae stood down on the grass, wringing her hands, watching helplessly. Tom straightened out Rebekah's limbs, and tilted her head back. After gently pushing down on her chin, he opened her mouth to check her airway, and found it clear. Kneeling over her, he placed the heel of his hand over her sternum just above her breastbone, locked the fingers of his other hand over it and gave thirty deep, rapid chest compressions, leaning his weight on his straightened arms. He heard Clara gasp, and he knew it was a shocking thing to witness. But he just kept going. After checking Rebekah's airway again, he gave her two quick rescue breaths before he resumed CPR, giving another thirty rapid compressions. He alternated this pattern, hearing a tune in his mind that helped to keep the rhythm going, and prayed the ambulance wouldn't take long.

Rhoda ran up, gasping that help was on the way, and stood with Lida Mae.

After several minutes, Tom heard a distant siren wailing, and someone cried, "Thank *Gott*! They're here!"

He kept up the CPR until one of the EMTs put a hand on his shoulder. "Okay, son, good work. I'll take over from here."

Tom nodded and staggered to his feet, sore everywhere. CPR was hard work. And he wasn't even sure whether it had been successful.

The first EMT, a muscular Black man with cornrow braids running down his back, pressed his fingers to Rebekah's neck, and he looked at Tom and smiled.

"I've got a pulse," he said. His partner, a small, blonde woman with a ponytail hanging out the back of her uniform cap, went to the ambulance and brought back the stretcher. The two of them lifted Rebekah's small form onto it, and tucked a blanket around her. They started wheeling her to the ambulance.

"We're taking her to Pomerene, in Millersburg," the man said. He helped load Rebekah, who was now wearing an oxygen mask, into the back of the ambulance. He climbed up inside with her, and his partner started to close the doors.

"Wait a second, Cindy," the man said. She looked at him curiously, but nodded. The man looked at Tom, who was having a hard time holding back tears of relief. "You did good, son. You saved her life. If you hadn't performed CPR until we got here, we'd have been too late." He nodded to his partner, who closed the back doors of the vehicle, then ran around to the front, climbed in and they took off toward the hospital, lights flashing and sirens blaring.

Everyone stood looking around at one another in shock.

"I want to go to the hospital," Obadiah finally croaked out.

Jackson and Clara looked at each other, then nodded. "Rhoda, would you please—" Clara began, but Rhoda interrupted, anticipating her mother's request.

"I'll call for a ride," she said, running to the barn.

Tom sat down on the edge of the porch. He couldn't believe he'd remembered how to perform CPR. Out of curiosity during his running around years, he'd taken a course, along with his brothers and a few of their church friends. But he'd never needed it until today. He concentrated on getting his own racing pulse under control. He hadn't noticed Lida Mae approaching until she nudged him, and he glumly hoped she wasn't going to say anything snarky; he didn't think he could take it right then. But she gave him an uncertain smile and handed him a glass of lemonade. "Here, you look like you could use this."

He took the glass and nodded his thanks. His mouth was parched. He gulped down the cold, sweet drink, and looked around for more. Lida Mae refilled his glass before filling glasses for the rest of them.

Rhoda ran back from the barn, and accepted a glass of lemonade from Lida Mae. "The ride will be here in twenty minutes," she said once she'd gulped down half a glass. She dropped down to sit on the edge of the porch beside Tom and Jackson, and after a moment, Lida Mae sat next to her. Obadiah and Clara sat in the rocking chairs.

"That was quite impressive," Jackson commented, shaking his head in wonder. "Where did you learn to do it? It's an *Englisch* thing, ain't so?"

Tom grimaced. "*Ja*, it is. But it's one of the things I feel we Amish should learn. Some progress is *gut*, *nee*?"

"I'd certainly say so," Obadiah said before pushing to his feet. "Thank you, Tom. I've dithered about my feelings for that stubborn old woman too long, and I almost lost her. If not for you…" The old man sniffed and scrubbed at his eyes. "I'm going in and getting ready to go to the hospital."

"I'll go with you, Obadiah," Jackson said after exchanging glances with Clara. The old man grunted his assent and pushed through the screen door.

Jackson put a hand on Tom's shoulder and squeezed, surprising the younger man. "Thank you from me, too. Rebekah is important to us around here."

Clara, Rhoda and even Lida Mae nodded in agreement, and Tom felt an odd squeezing in his chest. "*Denki*. If I helped save her, it was *Gott's* will, and He was working through me and my hands."

Rhoda looked at him with a new respect evident in her eyes. "Well, I'm going to find a course in town, and learn how to do that, too, before someone else needs it and all I can do is stand there, helplessly."

Lida Mae glanced almost shyly at Tom, causing him to do a double take. *What's that about?* She cleared her throat, and said, "There's a class coming up at the community center where I teach stained-glass art. We still have time to sign up."

Jackson, Clara and Rhoda all looked at her, then at each other. "I'm in," Rhoda said.

Her parents shrugged, and Clara said, "I think I'd like to learn, too. Do you think it's permitted, Jackson?"

He frowned a moment then he also shrugged. "Let's ask for forgiveness if it's not, after taking the class." He gave his wife a wry smile. "I don't want to ask for permission, just in case."

Tom saw Lida Mae and Rhoda exchange amazed glances, and he felt good about himself for the first time in weeks. He didn't know where he fit in in Charm, Ohio. But at least today, his being there had been a *gut* thing. Maybe a *Gott* thing.

Clara stood and dusted off her skirt. "Come, girls. It's time to go relieve your sister at the store. I'm feeling better, so I'll go help out. Lida Mae, you can stay and get supper ready."

A van pulled into the driveway, and Jackson jumped to his feet. "Clara, tell Obadiah the ride is here. I need to run inside and get my wallet." He leaned in and kissed his wife on the cheek, and she smiled softly at him and put a hand over the spot on her face.

Tom blushed and looked away, accidentally meeting Lida Mae's eyes. She said nothing, but he could tell she was amused by his reaction to seeing them display their affection that way. His parents didn't do that.

Jackson came back outside, wallet in hand, and met Obadiah at the van. Before climbing into the back, he called out to Tom. "Sorry I won't be here to help with the afternoon feeding, Tom. You okay without me?"

Tom heard Lida Mae, who was standing nearby, suck in some air, and looked at her. She looked ready to speak, then caught his eye, and closed her mouth, frowning. Tom felt as if he'd personally hurt her, when it was her father who had carelessly ignored the fact that his capable daughter was standing right there, eager to be asked to step in and help out in the barn. He realized that Jackson was waiting for him to answer, and waved with a forced smile. "Of course! Go do what you need to. We've got this."

Jackson nodded, not noticing Tom's use of the word "we," and closed the van door, and the vehicle pulled away, heading to the hospital. Clara, who was standing nearby, gave Tom a look that plainly said she had noticed his wording, and her daughter's unexpected restraint. She gave him a slight nod, which he interpreted to mean that this time, anyway, Lida Mae could help with the ranch and farm chores.

"This time," Clara said. "Because of the circumstances."

Tom turned to look at Lida Mae, who was regarding him curiously. "We?"

He nodded decisively. "*Ja*, we. If you'll help, that is. Fact is, you grew up working this spread, and your *dat* said you're really *gut* at it. So, will you stay and help?"

She narrowed her eyes at him, then, after exchanging a look with her *maem*, gave a slow nod. He thought he might even see a smile lurking somewhere in her sharp, green eyes—but he couldn't be certain. He'd take what he could get as far as a peace treaty with Lida Mae.

Rhoda came outside and called to her sister. "Are you ready to head to town?"

"I'm going to go back with you after all," Clara said decisively. "I'm feeling better, and Lida Mae will stay here and help Tom with the chores, before getting supper started."

Rhoda's eyebrows shot toward her hairline, but she recovered quickly and gave Clara a smile. "Okay! I'll pull the buggy around while you grab your things, *Maem*!"

Clara looked at Lida Mae and said, "Don't think this means I've changed my mind, daughter. But needs must. And Tom's right. You are quite gut at the farm work." She looked distressed for a moment, then met her daughter's eyes. "It's just not the life I want for you, my *lieb*."

Before Lida Mae could respond, Clara hurried inside to fetch her bag, bonnet and a lightweight shawl. Then she climbed into the buggy and she and Rhoda drove away, leaving Lida Mae and Tom alone.

Tom gave Lida Mae a cautious look. "Um, do we have a truce?"

She tilted her head, causing the strings of her *kapp* to

sway gently. Then she threw back her head and burst into a peal of loud, unexpected laughter.

Tom stared at her, wondering what on Earth had possessed her. After a minute she got herself under control and wiped her eyes. "Oh, I'm sorry. I'm not laughing at you, Tom. I think I had to release some tension! What a day!"

He nodded. "You can say that again."

She considered him a moment. "Tom, I'm sorry we got off to such a rough start. And I'm not going to lie and tell you I'm happy you're here, because, stolen life—whether you meant to or not. But I will say I know it's not your fault. I don't know what your story is—I do want to hear it, but not right now, okay? But you being here isn't what's keeping me from doing what I want. It's my parents' old-fashioned ideas of a woman's place in Amish society. And if you left tomorrow, they'd just find some other man to do the farm and ranch work. Until I can change their minds about that, which I don't see happening any time soon, I guess I'm going to have to accept their decision." She looked at him closely, then shook her head. "But now I'm being selfish. I may be resigned to my fate, but that doesn't mean you are. Look, I need to change into my barn clothes and we have to get the chores done so I can start supper—you know, proper women's work." He thought her eyes twinkled a bit at this. "But maybe later you can tell me how you ended up here in Ohio, when clearly, you'd rather be in Texas. Okay?"

He felt a lightening in his shoulders as tension slowly seeped from them. And a gladness entered his heart. He might not want to marry this puzzle of a woman, but he was starting to think maybe he wouldn't mind having her as a friend.

He nodded. "*Ja*, let's get the chores done, and then I'll help you make supper while I fill you in on my sad tale. Deal?"

Her mouth popped open in surprise. "You'll help make supper? You can cook?"

He shrugged. "My *mudder* has no daughters. So she taught her sons to cook. She said we might need to know how if we couldn't convince anybody to marry us."

She laughed, and he saw the same gladness in her eyes that he was feeling. He knew this didn't mean they were going to become friends overnight, but it was better—much better—than what he'd been living with. He'd take it. And he suspected she was just as relieved to clear the air a bit. Her next words confirmed it.

"Then I accept your offer, Tom. And I'm looking forward to hearing your story. Maybe between us, we can figure out how you can get back home to your ranch and your family."

He offered a tentative smile. "*Ja*, and how you can get back to doing the work you love."

Her face fell, and she signed. But then she rallied and gave a small smile. "Well, you never know, right? I'm praying that *Gott* will help me do that, Tom, and keep on doing my stained-glass art, too. And with Him, anything is possible, *nee*?"

He nodded. "Oh, *ja*. Anything at all."

He wondered for a moment about her stained-glass art. He'd yet to see any of it, but it sounded interesting.

She studied his face a moment. "You really believe that?"

What could she mean by that? Didn't she believe? He nodded slowly. "*Ja*, of course I do. Why, don't you?"

After a moment she gave a decisive nod. "I do. Sometimes it is a challenge, but my faith is strong. I do believe, Tom, *denki*."

Before she could leave, he caught her hand in his. Her eyebrows shot upward, but she didn't pull away. "Lida Mae, I'm promising here and now that if it's in my power, I will help you. Do you believe me?"

She cocked her head to one side and considered him a moment. "*Ja*, actually I do. And I'll return that promise, Tom. I'm not sure how yet, but I'll figure it out."

She turned and headed inside to change, and Tom frowned after her. Seeing this new, unexpected side of Lida Mae, he wasn't completely certain he was sorry that the small, dainty and very predictable girly girl back in Texas had dumped him before their courtship got off the ground. Next to Lida Mae, she was kind of drab and boring.

"*Ach*, now I'm getting all *ferhoodled*. I'm just going to be glad that the woman has decided I'm not her enemy—at least for now—and we can go from there. And if she can help me figure out how to get back home where I belong, so much the better."

Chapter Four

The next few days passed quietly, and Lida Mae thought maybe she and Tom had achieved a sort of détente. She admitted to herself this was probably because they simply didn't see much of each other. Permission for her to work in the barn had not been repeated, so the only place they saw each other regularly was at meals. She hadn't had a chance to talk with him privately, so she still hadn't heard his side of the story about how he ended up working on her family spread. She felt a bit more tolerant of him after their brief talk, but until she heard more, she could not help harbor some negative feelings, even if she suspected he was as much a victim of circumstance as she.

She understood why she was disposed to resent his presence; that made sense, since he'd shown up out of nowhere and basically stolen her life, whether he'd meant to or not. She was starting to suspect the later, but until she heard his story, the jury was out.

But Lida Mae had been raised to be pleasant and welcoming, and by nature was a friendly person who enjoyed the company of others. Her gut deep antipathy toward Tom went beyond what she could excuse by their circumstances, and she didn't understand it. This puzzled and bothered her, which in turn caused her to be even more irritated with the Texan.

She was attempting not to be openly rude or hostile, and despite their truce, it wasn't easy.

To that end, she had been spending a lot of time in town, either at the quilt shop or the community center. She and her mother and sisters were quilting a white-on-white king-size quilt someone had commissioned as a wedding gift, and the deadline for completing it was fast approaching. It was snowy white cotton with a hand-stitched feather design all over it, and it was extremely labor-intensive and hard on the eyes.

It was midafternoon not quite a week after Rebekah's heart attack, and all four of the Beiler women were seated around the quilt frame, rapidly taking tiny stitches over the stenciled pattern of large, fluffy plumes that covered the quilt. When working with a white quilt, they didn't dare eat or drink at the frame, even though the finished product would be washed to remove the stencil before being delivered to the customer.

Clara pushed back from the frame and set her needle into the fabric, then stood with a groan, her hand pressing her lower back. "*Ach!* This one is a bear! I need a break, girls. My back aches."

"Go have something to eat and drink, *Maem*," Rhoda suggested. "We've got this."

"Yes, it's nearly finished now, thank *Gott*!" Priscilla said, standing and stretching in place. "I believe I'll join you in that break, though, *Maem*."

"I could use a break, but I really want to finish," Rhoda said. "We start CPR tomorrow night, remember? We'll need to finish in time to get home for an early dinner if we're to make it to class on time."

"Oh, *ja*, I'd forgotten that!" Clara said.

Rhoda snickered. "I heard that the bishop and his *fraa* signed up. He's an old friend of Obadiah's, and that old man has been praising Tom and his CPR to anyone who will listen."

Clara looked arrested by the idea. "Well! I guess we'll see tomorrow. Now, do stop for a bit, Lida Mae. Your back must ache."

Lida Mae reluctantly set her needle into the fabric, and stood up. "Oof, you're right, *Maem*. I am a bit stiff."

"Well, we've been sitting here for three hours, so no wonder!" Rhoda winked at her sister. "Come on. I brought some quiche from home. I'll heat it up."

"Oh, yum!" Priscilla exclaimed. "I'll make a fresh pot of *kaffi*." The two hurried toward the kitchenette in the back of the store, leaving Lida Mae and her *maem* to wander up front.

"Good thing business has been slow today," Lida Mae said, automatically straightening bolts of fabric as she made her way toward the front. "We've been able to get a lot done."

"*Ja*, you're right. And even though this quilt will be gorgeous when it's finished, I don't mind telling you I hope not to work on another white-on-white quilt anytime soon. It's too hard on my old eyes!"

Lida Mae rolled her own green eyes at her *maem's* dramatic statement. "*Maem*, you're not even fifty yet."

"You raise three daughters and spend forty years peering at tiny quilt stitches, and then tell me your eyes don't feel old when you're forty-seven."

Lida Mae chuckled, but privately she doubted she'd be raising any children in the near future. Until *Gott* decided it was time for her to meet a man who made her feel the way her parents obviously still felt about each other, she wasn't interested.

She gave an unconscious sigh, attracting her mother's keen eye. Showing the uncanny gift she'd always had for seemingly reading her daughters' minds, she walked over and gave her youngest a spontaneous hug, squeezing tight. "Give it time, my child. Everything has its season, remember."

Lida Mae found herself blinking back sudden tears. She sniffed and returned her *mudder's* hug, then stood back and swiped a tear from her cheek.

"Oh, honey, I'm sorry you're so unhappy right now. I never meant to ruin your life." Her mother clutched her apron in both hands and looked truly dismayed. "It's just that I fear you'll be alone all your life if you keep doing men's work on the farm. We need the young men of the community to see that you're also competent and capable in the kitchen so they'll overlook the fact that you're several inches taller than most of them."

Lida Mae blinked back more tears, feeling blessed to have a mother who clearly loved her and cared for her happiness. Why couldn't she also understand that after setting the example of a marriage based on faith and love, her parents had ruined their daughters for anything less?

"Oh, *Maem*, I don't want a man who settles for me because I can make *gut* pancakes and meatloaf despite my freakish height. I want a man who will love me for who I am, and welcome my contributions both in the house and on the farm." Furiously wiping at the unwelcome tears, she blurted, "Why aren't there any tall Amish men in this community? *Dat* is much taller than I am! If *Gott* made me this way, why isn't He sending me a man who will appreciate me for who I am?"

Her mother, tears in her own brown eyes, reached again for her daughter, but Lida Mae held out a hand. "*Maem*, it's alright. I understand you and *Dat* are acting from love. I just need time. But if you hug me again, I'm going to lose my composure. Why don't you go get your lunch, and I'll take a couple minutes up here to collect myself. Then I'll join you. Will we eat outside on the deck?"

Worry still clear in her eyes, Clara nodded. "*Ja*, *gut* idea, as it's a lovely day. If you're sure you want to be alone?"

Lida Mae nodded. "Please. Just five minutes."

"I'll see you out back."

Lida Mae began picking up items people had shelved improperly while browsing.

Her arms were soon full of fat quarters in various colors and prints, and she snagged a tomato-shaped pincushion from the floor, shaking her head at how messy people could be.

A tinkling bell alerted Lida Mae that someone was entering the shop, and she stepped out from behind the shelves, a polite smile on her lips and a greeting on the tip of her tongue; but instead of a customer, there stood Tom.

With a squeak of surprise, she dropped the pincushion, which rolled toward Tom, stopping halfway between them.

Feeing a surge of unexpected pleasure at encountering Lida Mae, and hoping to hide the rush of heat to his cheeks, Tom moved to retrieve the pin cushion at the same moment Lida Mae said, "Oops! I'll get it."

They bumped heads, and Lida Mae yelped in pain and promptly fell right onto her *hinnerdale*, tossing fat quarters all over the floor.

"Oh, no!" Tom cried, stepping forward to help her, but instead he slipped when his foot came down on the round pincushion. After flailing his arms for a moment, he went down on his own rump.

Tom sat there rubbing his head and blinking at Lida Mae, who was rubbing her own head and staring back at Tom. The offending pincushion had shot off in another direction and was nowhere in sight.

"Drat!" Lida Mae said, then covered her mouth with one hand, as if she'd said something much worse.

Tom couldn't help himself. He felt the full weight of their ridiculous situation—not just their present predicament, either—and it all seemed hilarious suddenly. Here they were, two mature adults, acting like a pair of *bopplin*.

A snort escaped from Tom, and he covered his own mouth, eyes wide as he looked at Lida Mae, expecting her to be pretty irritated with him. But she stared back, and to his surprise and relief he saw the corners of her lips quirk upward, and a giggle escaped her. The next moment, they were both sitting on the floor, laughing uproariously, tears leaking from their eyes.

"Lida Mae? What on earth is going on?" Clara's voice called from the back of the shop.

A moment later, she and Lida Mae's sisters rounded the display and stopped short at the sight of Tom and Lida Mae sitting on the floor, laughing.

Priscilla shook her head. "I think they've lost their wits."

Tom pushed to his feet and reached a hand down to help Lida Mae to hers. She looked reluctant to accept his hand, and he rolled his eyes at her. "What, are you afraid I'm not strong enough to help one *maedel* up from the floor?"

With a sheepish smile, she accepted the offered hand and he hauled her upright with ease, almost causing her to overcorrect and tip right into him.

He put out his hands to steady her, but she regained her balance, and he saw heat creeping across her cheeks. He thought that was mighty interesting, but quickly shook the idea out of his head. He didn't want to risk their fragile truce by getting ideas into his head about her.

Remember your aim is to get back home, Tom! Not to find reasons to stay in Ohio. But at the moment, he couldn't recall exactly what it was about staying in Ohio that he was so against. Glancing at the floor, he saw the fat quarters still scattered about and bent to collect them at the same time as Lida Mae said, "I've got those."

"Watch out!" Rhoda cried, and both Tom and Lida Mae jerked upright just before they suffered another collision.

"That's what happened before," Lida Mae said sheepishly as she watched Tom gather up the fabric bundles, which he handed to her with a pained smile.

"*Ja*, sorry about that. Now, where did that pincushion go? Ah! There it is." He picked up the slightly squashed tomato pincushion and offered it to Lida Mae.

"Yep, that's the one that took you down," Lida Mae said.

She cleared her throat. "So what brought you here before the runaway pin cushion caused all that trouble?"

Tom scrambled to recall what he had come in for, then he nodded. "Right. Clara, Jackson sent me to tell you he's riding with Obadiah to the rehabilitation center tonight to visit Rebekah. He said not to wait dinner on him, as he'll eat while they visit."

Claire nodded. "*Denki*, Tom. I'll see you tonight at supper."

He glanced at Lida Mae, who gave him an uncertain smile. Then he nodded respectfully at Clara. "I'll see you later. I'm headed to the hardware store in Berlin now—Orme's. Do you need anything?"

"Oh! *Ja*, I've actually got a short list of things I need in the back. Do you mind waiting a moment?"

"Not at all."

"I'll only be a minute." Clara hurried toward the back of the store, leaving Tom and the three sisters waiting by the front door.

"Well," Rhoda said, a teasing gleam in her eyes, "It's certainly nice seeing the two of you getting along better. Isn't it, Prissy?"

Priscilla held up her hands as if warding off trouble. "Don't pull me into this! I don't want to find a field mouse in my bed."

Lida Mae gasped in outrage. "Rhoda! Priscilla! Stop!"

Tom thought that the look Lida Mae cast at her older sisters should have the smaller women quaking in their shoes. But they only laughed.

"Please!" Rhoda chuckled. "I've waited a long time to tease you about a man." She looked at Tom. "No offense, Tom. Lida Mae can be a bit of a grump. That's all I mean."

Tom wasn't so sure that was true, but a glance at Lida Mae convinced him he didn't want to pursue that; at least not here or now. Fortunately, Clara returned before anything else could be said, and Tom accepted a short list of things she needed from the hardware store.

"Okay, I'll add these to my list, and I'll see you all at supper." He chanced another look in Lida Mae's direction, but found her studying the squashed pin cushion she still held. She didn't meet his eyes, and he signed inwardly, hoping her sisters hadn't undone any progress he and she had made in their very new and fragile friendship. He felt regret tug at him at the possibility.

Nothing I can do about it now. Maybe I can catch her later and tell her my story. I'll try after supper.

Feeling a bit more optimistic, he gave a wave, turned and left the shop.

Lida Mae waited for the door to close behind Tom, then, furious, rounded on her sisters. "I cannot believe you two purposely embarrassed me in front of Tom like that! Why would you do that?"

Clara narrowed her eyes at her elder two daughters, who had the grace to look repentant. "Did you do that? Shame on you both."

"Sorry, Lida Mae," they both murmured.

"It's just nice to see you laughing with a boy," Rhoda said. "I didn't mean anything, honest."

"Well, I hope he knows that," Lida Mae groused. "We're just starting to get along."

Priscilla looked interested at that. "Do you want to get along with Tom, Lida Mae?"

All three older Beiler women waited for Lida Mae's answer, and she pursed her lips, considering. Did she?

I do. Oh, sis yuscht. *This isn't* gut! *Is it? I'm so confused!*

To the eagerly waiting women she merely said, "Maybe. Isn't it better if we get along than fight all the time? Besides, what's the use? I have to accept the decision of my parents, like the filial *maedel* I am. Now, if you'll excuse me, I'm going to eat my lunch and then get back to work on that quilt."

She had the satisfaction of leaving them all staring after her, speechless, as she marched toward the back of the shop to get her lunch. That made a nice change, anyway!

Chapter Five

Lida Mae and her family exited the big classroom at the Charm Community Center. "I feel better knowing that if someone has a heart attack around me I'll be ready to do something to help. I felt so helpless when it happened to Rebekah," she said.

"*Ja*, me, too. Thank *Gott* Tom was there," Clara said.

They had all just completed a Red Cross community CPR course, which taught them the basics of keeping someone having a heart attack alive until help arrived.

"Do you think it's interfering in *Gott's* will, though?" Priscilla asked tentatively. "If they would have died without intervention?"

"I don't think it's any different from going to the hospital to get stitches, or taking medications to control a health condition," Lida Mae said.

"That's a question for the bishop," Clara said. "What do you say, Ben?"

"I confess I was skeptical at first," Ben Lapp, the bishop of their community, said from up ahead where he and his wife, Sally, were walking next to Lida Mae's parents. "Not about CPR interfering with *Gott's* will, but more about whether it was something we Amish wanted to do. But Sally and I were so impressed by Obadiah's account of how you stepped right in and kept Rebekah alive until the EMTs got there, Tom, that I decided this was a *gut* idea. I consulted the other community elders, and we prayed about it. Eventually we all agreed that it was not against *Gott's* will to do something to help someone stay alive, nor was it against the *Ordnung*, so here we are."

"I didn't think it was even that fancy, to be honest," Jackson said. "Except maybe for that AED machine. I'm not sure I'd be comfortable using one of those."

"*Ja*, it's a little intimidating," Ben agreed. "However, I've learned that other Amish communities have even put AEDs in some public spaces. That's something I'll have to think and pray about."

A few steps behind their elders, Lida Mae grinned at her sisters and whispered, "Well, the song they had us singing to keep rhythm was pretty fancy, though."

Rhoda and Priscilla giggled and nodded their agreement. The song recommended by the Red Cross for people to keep in their heads while doing CPR, "Staying Alive" by the Bee Gees, was probably not anything any Amish person who hadn't had their running-around years back in the 1970s would know.

Tom, who had been walking ahead with some of the older members of their community, dropped back to walk with the Beiler sisters. "Y'all looked as if you were catching on pretty well."

Priscilla grimaced. "I'm pretty sure I could do it if I needed to, but Lida Mae is a natural! Her height and reach really gave her an advantage."

"It's not like I had anything to do with my size," Lida Mae muttered.

"No, but *Gott* did, and if He thought you needed to be so tall, there must be a reason," Priscilla pointed out.

Lida Mae's mouth quirked. "That's fair. And it did come in handy tonight! So… I think I'll stick around for a bit and get some work done on my stained-glass project here. I'll get a ride home later." Priscilla frowned. "But I think I heard *Dat* suggest we all go get ice cream now. You know you love ice cream!"

"Aw, Lida Mae, come out with all of us," Rhoda coaxed. "It'll be fun!"

Lida Mae felt conflicted. She surely did love ice cream, and it was always fun going out with her family. But she really needed to get the piece of stained glass she was using as a sample for her next class done. "Ach! What a choice! I really want to go, but I have to get this project done." She chewed on her lip, trying to think when she could get back to the community center if not that evening.

Clara, who had dropped back from the other elders without her daughters noticing, heard Lida Mae's comment, and, frowning, stopped and waited for them to catch up. "What's this I hear, Lida Mae? You don't want to go for ice cream with us?"

Lida Mae sighed. "I hate to miss out, *Maem*, but if it's okay with you and *Dat*. I need to work on the stained-glass piece I'll be using as an example for my students."

"But you'll be here alone," Clara protested.

Tom, who had stood quietly by with Priscilla and Rhoda during the conversation, cleared his throat. "Clara, if it's okay with you, I could drive Lida Mae home."

Clara looked at Tom in surprise. "Really? You don't want ice cream?"

Tom shrugged. "I drove myself. I don't mind helping her out."

Clara smiled at Tom. "*Denki*, then. I suppose that's fine, but don't be late."

Rhoda turned and waggled her eyebrows at Lida Mae, who stuck her tongue out at her older sister before turning to look at Tom.

He was grinning at her.

"What?"

He shook his head. "Nothing, it's just that your interaction with your sisters reminds me of mine with my brothers. It's nice."

She found herself caught by his direct gaze, and swallowed nervously. "You must miss them a lot, I guess."

He nodded. "*Ja*, I really do. We grew up together doing everything together. It feels very strange not having them beside me while I work with the horses or do the chores."

She considered that for a moment, and realized that if she found herself a thousand miles from home, living with strangers, not seeing her parents and sisters and her little nephew Danny regularly, she would feel lost indeed. "I hadn't thought about how lonely you must be for home. I'm sorry, Tom."

They stood a moment more looking at each other before Lida Mae shook her head to snap herself out of it. "Well, come on then, my classroom is down this way." She gave him a small, encouraging smile before turning and heading down the hall.

Tom fell into step beside her, and sent her a sideways smile. "I was thinking that we could swing past the Scoop Shack on the way home and grab a couple cones for the road."

She smiled reluctantly and shook her head. "I admit I like the way you think. If you let me pay for your cone,

I won't feel as guilty for making you wait around for me here."

"Are you kidding? I can't wait to see your set up here. I've heard about your stained glass from your sisters, and you've mentioned it a time or two. I'm looking forward to it. But I won't argue if you insist on buying me ice cream." At her raised eyebrow, he chuckled. "Hey, it's not every day a pretty *maedel* offers to buy me a treat. I'd be a fool to say no."

"It only seems fair." As they neared the classroom, she thought about the fact that she didn't mind Tom coming to see her glass operation. He didn't seem to see it as a waste of time, like some of the young Amish men she knew. A warm feeling stole over her as she realized she was looking forward to showing her passion for glass art to Tom.

And isn't that interesting? But he's going back to Texas. I need to make sure that I don't start getting the wrong idea about this Texas cowboy and farmer. Because the one thing he has made very clear is that he doesn't plan to stick around Charm, Ohio, any longer than he has to.

The thought made her rather sad; a feeling she tried to ignore as she dug the key to the classroom out of her pocket and unlocked the door.

As Tom followed, he couldn't help admiring the easy, graceful way she moved; her athletic form clad in a modest green dress and black apron, her hair tucked into her prayer *kapp*. On her feet were white tennis shoes. He had to admit she made quite a picture.

She flipped on the lights, and Tom looked around curiously, taking in the space.

There were two long tables with electrical outlets

placed at regular intervals underneath, workstations all along their lengths.

Along one wall were sturdy-looking wooden cubbies filled with a rainbow of glass in various sizes. Fascinated, he wandered over to look at it, reaching out to run a finger along the edge of a purple sheet of clear glass.

"Don't touch that."

He quickly pulled back his finger, and surreptitiously sucked a bead of blood off the tip where the sharp edge had sliced his skin just before Lida Mae's warning. He turned to find her smiling at him. "You'll cut yourself."

He examined the small cut, and found it had already stopped bleeding. "It's nothing."

She gave a one-shouldered shrug and walked over to what he assumed must be her personal work area. It consisted of a table with a large space for creating glass art, along with a fascinating array of tools. On the table's surface was a work-in-progress. He walked over to have a look.

"Is that a quilt block made of glass?"

"*Ja*. It's what I do." She glanced at him sideways. "You probably think it's fancy and a foolish waste of my time. Most of the Amish men I know think so."

He looked at her and wondered why such a talented, interesting woman had such low self-esteem. "Is that what you think?"

She blinked at him, obviously caught off-guard by his question. "Well, of course not. It's my art. Why would I do it if I thought it was a waste of time?"

He cocked his head and looked at the glass creation. "It's a double-wedding-ring quilt block, ain't so?"

"That's right."

"My *maem* quilts. And she and my *dat* have a quilt like this on their bed, only in different colors."

Lida Mae studied the block, which was made of many curved pieces in various textures of red and green glass, with a small, satisfied smile on her face.

Tom thought she might well look satisfied. He imagined cutting the glass into those curves was not easy.

"Surely this is no beginner piece."

Curiously, she regarded him, one eyebrow cocked. "*Nee?* Why do you say that?"

He frowned down at the creation. "Well… I'd have to say the curved pieces of glass would be too difficult for a beginner to achieve."

She nodded. "Very good. You're right. This isn't my classroom piece. It's one I'm working on to sell in the quilt shop."

He looked at her in surprise. "You make these to sell? My *maem* would absolutely love one of these! Do you take custom orders?"

"Like, another wedding-ring block?"

"*Ja*, but in the colors of their wedding quilt."

She pursed her lips, drawing his attention to them. He blinked. *No, Tom. Do not go there! Don't you have enough trouble? Remember your goal!*

Apparently oblivious to the unwelcome direction his thoughts had taken, she nodded slowly. "I guess I could. But I have a couple other things to finish first. Are you in a big hurry?"

He focused on her words instead of her lips. "Um, no."

"What colors?"

He looked at the wall of glass and walked over to point at a violet sheet, and then, after a short search, he pointed at a peach sheet of glass.

She followed and examined his choices. "I like those together. I have some in those colors with more interesting textures. These is the beginner glass. My glass is in the closed cabinets." They walked over, and she unlocked a cabinet and threw open the doors for him to take a look.

He gave a low whistle. "Wow, you've got a nice collection."

"I bought this with what they pay me to teach the class. I've got another, smaller work area at home in an outbuilding I share with one of my sisters and our *dat*. There's some glass there, and a few tools. But this is most of it." She considered her collection of glass in all colors and textures, and several different sizes. Some seemed to gleam like jewels. "I may have a little bit of a hoarder problem." She cast him a sideways glance, and he thought there was a twinkle in her eyes. She pulled out some glass for him to consider. Soon they had settled on the glass for his mother's quilt block. She set aside the sheets in an empty slot, and closed and locked the cabinet. "My classroom piece is over here, if you'd like to see it."

Does she sound shy? Or am I imagining things?

Tom followed Lida Mae to another table, and saw a much simpler piece—a white star on a deep blue background. The star gleamed with hidden colors. There was copper wrapping edging all the glass pieces.

"This is beautiful, the way it changes color as I move around it."

"It's opalescent. It's been treated with something to give it that effect. I really like it, too. And the lines are straight and short—simple for beginners."

"What do you still need to do with it?"

"I need to solder the pieces together. See, it's just laid out, but not connected yet."

"But you've got metal on it. It's not soldered?"

"*Nee.* That's what comes next."

He watched as she plugged in a soldering iron, which was tucked into what looked like a big metal spring to keep it off the table.

She picked up a bottle of something labeled Liquid Flux, and poured some into the bottle's cap, then set aside the bottle. She plucked a small paintbrush from a mug and dipped it into the cap, then began painting the liquid all over the copper between all the pieces of glass, including the sides.

When she was finished, she put the brush back in the mug and picked up the soldering wire and the soldering iron. "I'm going to tack it down to hold it all together first."

She melted little drops of solder all over the piece, joining all the pieces of glass together. "Now, that's not going anywhere."

Tom was seriously impressed. "How did you learn to do this?"

"I took a class a few years ago right here. I fell in love with the process." She blushed a bit and looked away, as if afraid she'd revealed too much. He turned away to hide a smile. So the girl was vulnerable after all. But he knew that, after hearing her tearfully begging her father not to take away the farmwork she loved.

He watched as she removed some pins that had been holding the pieces together, and said, "Now, I'll do a simple flat solder."

"What's that?"

"Watch."

She touched the tip of the soldering iron to the solder, and spread it along the copper, as if she was painting. "You make that look easy," he said in wonder. "I'll bet it's not."

"I have plenty of experience."

"How hot is that iron?"

"It's eleven hundred degrees Fahrenheit."

His mouth dropped open. "Yikes! You wouldn't want to accidentally touch that!"

"You wouldn't want to accidentally touch the blade of a saw while it's in motion, either, or a pitchfork tine while it's tossing hay."

He considered that. "*Gut* point."

She smiled, and quickly finished flat-soldering the piece.

"Are you finished?"

"*Nee.* That's the first part. Next comes the bead soldering. It's much slower. The students have a lot of trouble with this part at first."

She showed him how to hold the iron at an angle, with the soldering wire behind it, and slowly move it along the flat solders, creating a nice, uniform look. Once it was done, she waited a minute, then flipped it over. Glancing up at him, she said, "Would you like to try?"

He shoved his hands into his pockets and shook his head. "*Nee*, I don't want to risk ruining your class sample."

She pursed her lips, but shrugged and did the same thing to the back side.

Finally, she turned the piece on its side and, after fluxing it, laid down solder along the sides of the piece. Then she set it down to cool.

Finished, she surveyed her work. "That will do," she murmured.

She looked at him, and when she found him staring at her with an enigmatic smile, asked, "What?"

"Sorry. I'm just amazed at your skills. I wish I could do that."

"I could teach you. Why don't you take my class?"

"I couldn't." He paused. "Could I?"

She shrugged. "Why not? It seems to me a guy who isn't afraid to take a CPR class wouldn't be afraid to take a stained-glass class."

He considered that for a moment. "You're right. I might do that."

When he didn't look away after a few seconds, Lida Mae squirmed a bit. "What?"

He shrugged. "Oh, I was just thinking about how we're actually pretty similar."

She rested against the table and cocked her head at an angle. "How so?"

"As you pointed out, I took CPR, which isn't something you see a lot of our folks doing. And here you are, doing something else that doesn't really fit into the typical Amish mold. I guess we're both a couple of rebels at heart."

"Don't let my *dat* and *maem* hear you say that!" But he thought her eyes looked softer as she regarded him. His own eyes dropped to her lips, which also looked very soft. And inviting.

Yanking his eyes back to hers, he forced a casual smile. "So! Are you ready for some ice cream?"

As if relieved to change the subject, Lida Mae nodded. "Oh, *ja*, you don't have to ask me twice now that my work here is done. Let's go. I'm pretty hungry."

Outside, they walked to Tom's buggy and were soon headed down the road toward home. She didn't try to make conversation, so he kept his own council. When they reached the Scoop Shack, he guided the horse into the driveway, and up to a hitching rack. He turned to her. "Are you still buying?"

"Of course! Especially now that I'm adding a cheeseburger and fries to my ice cream order."

Tom's stomach rumbled at the thought, and Lida Mae giggled. "That was pretty loud. Maybe I'd better buy you more than ice cream, too."

"Only if you let me buy next time."

He winced, wondering if she'd think he was asking her out. But when he glanced at her, she didn't seem to have taken any notice of the comment.

"Why would I ever say no to that?" She grinned and walked up to the ordering window, where a teenager with spiky blue hair and a nose ring nodded at Lida Mae and gave Tom a curious look. When it was their turn, Tom ordered a cheeseburger and fresh cut fries, along with a double-dip chocolate sundae with extra butterscotch sauce and two cherries.

Lida Mae ordered her own burger and fries, and a strawberry sundae with whipped cream and strawberry sauce. "Hold the peanuts please, Buela," she added as an afterthought.

Buela nodded. "Gotcha. Your folks and sisters were here a bit ago."

"*Ja*, I had to finish something up at the community center."

Buela nodded and cracked her gum. "Gotcha." She sent another considering look toward Tom, then turned back to Lida Mae. "Okay, the order will be right up, Lida Mae."

When their food arrived, she pulled out her wallet and paid for both, tucking several dollars into the tip jar, which gained her a smile and an enthusiastic gum crack from Buela.

They sat at a picnic table near their buggy and tucked into their meal.

He studied her for a moment. So, do you want to hear my sad tale?

Lida Mae popped a fry into her mouth and nodded. "*Ja*, if you want to tell me."

He realized, to his surprise, that he really did want to share with this lovely, prickly girl who was starting, despite his best efforts to the contrary, to get under his skin. And he kind of owed it to her, since her *dat* had shared her story without her knowledge. Tom grimaced a bit at the thought that Lida Mae would probably not be thrilled to know Jackson had overshared with him on the topic of his youngest daughter's—at least for the moment—squashed hopes and dreams.

I hope she never finds out about that!

He took a big bite of his chocolate sundae to give himself a few moments to think where to start. A glance at Lida Mae showed that she was enjoying her own ice cream treat while waiting patiently for him to begin.

"Okay, you know I have two *brudders*, one older and one younger, *ja*?"

At her nod, he continued. "Of course you remember, since you met us all when your family visited our spread in Texas. So, we all grew up working the family ranch and farm together with our *dat*. We make a great team, and we figured we'd always be a team. But it turned out that our parents had different ideas."

He went on to explain that they had decided to leave everything to their oldest son, Paul, leaving Tom and Jake, the youngest brother, to find other positions.

Lida Mae froze with her spoon halfway to her mouth. "So, essentially, they stole your lives from you. Just like my parents did to me."

She's right. That's exactly what they did! And ja, it's exactly what her own parents did. We do have a lot in common, me and this fiery-haired maedel.

He nodded. "Yep, that about sums it up. My youngest brudder, Jake, is missing an arm. I don't know if you knew that. He lost it in a tracktor rollover when he was twelve."

"I do believe I heard that. So, can he still work the ranch and farm?"

Tom nodded. "Oh, *ja*! He's a wonder. He's a better farmer and rancher than most able-bodied men I know. In fact, he's able bodied—just missing an arm. I'd hire him any day."

"So has he found another job?"

"*Nee*. Others, even members of our own *gmay*, are apparently afraid to take a chance on a one-armed cowboy."

She frowned fiercely. "People from your own church community won't give him a chance? Well, that's not very Christian!"

He smiled at her defense of a near-stranger. This woman would make a true and valuable friend, he could see. "Not very. So that's why I'm determined to return to Texas, and why the three of us haven't given up hope yet that our folks will change their minds. I mean, they can't honestly mean for Jake to end up with nowhere to go, can they?"

He felt a bit lost at the thought, and seemingly without realizing what she was doing Lida Mae responded instinctively to his need by reaching out and capturing his hand in hers.

"Tom, I can see how difficult all this has been on you

and your *brudders*. At least my folks aren't saying I have to leave and find my own way. It's hard for me to fathom."

Afraid that if he spoke he might cry, Tom bit his lips and simply nodded. She continued. "I really believe that *Gott* is holding all of you in His hands, though, and that everything will work out for the best. Sometimes when I pray, I don't ask for a specific outcome to a situation. Instead, I just ask Gott to decide whatever would be best for me and everyone else and to make that happen. And you know something?"

She smiled into his eyes and he shook his head. "What?"

She gave a decisive nod. "That's usually what happens, Tom. *Gott* knows what we need. Let's pray together for a minute that *Gott* will make whatever is best happen for you and your *brudders, ja*?"

Tom had to blink his eyes hard for a few moments before he could nod his consent. They bowed their heads, and each prayed silently for *Gott* to help guide Tom, Jake and Paul to whatever course of action would be best for them.

When he was finished, Tom looked at Lida Mae, who was smiling back at him sympathetically. "Well!" she said, apparently realizing she still held his hand and quickly pulling it away. "Now you just need to wait and see what *Gott* decides to do! It's part of the adventure, ain't so?"

"Adventure?"

She laughed. "*Ja*, the adventure of life, Tom." Then she gave a sheepish chuckle. "And this is advice I also need to take, don't I?"

He returned her smile and nodded.

"It would seem so."

She pushed to her feet and tossed her trash into a nearby garbage can. "Well then, at least we both know what's next!"

He also stood and threw away his trash, and they started back to the buggy. "We do?"

"Of course! We know we have to trust *Gott* to help us figure it out."

With another laugh, he nodded. "That we do, Lida Mae. Meanwhile, I might just sign up for that stained glass class you mentioned."

She looked surprised. "Really? You might?"

"Sure, why wouldn't I?"

She gave a self-conscious shrug. "You'd be the first Amish man to do so."

"Huh. Well, I guess I have to agree with your sisters then."

They climbed into the buggy. "About what?"

He took up the reins and looked at her before driving off. "That the men around here are pretty *dumm*!"

Lida Mae's laughter colored the air with joy as the buggy headed toward the Beiler ranch, and Tom found himself feeling better than he had in weeks; since he'd left Texas.

What does that mean? Who knows. Just enjoy the ride, Tom, and let Gott *set the course.* Whether that would be back to Texas or not was a question that was growing larger in Tom's mind day by day.

Chapter Six

Rebekah was allowed to return home, with the understanding that she would not do any heavy housework, lifting, yard or barn chores.

Lida Mae intended to go over and see what help she might need, possibly the following afternoon, when she wasn't scheduled to work in the quilt shop.

Jackson and Tom were busy working with the two- and three-year-old Belgians, getting them used to responding to commands and working with humans, though they wouldn't be able to do any actual heavy hauling until they were fully mature, around four or five years old.

As a result of having many of her accustomed daily tasks removed from her responsibility, she found herself running out of things to do by midafternoon on days she didn't work in the quilt shop. It seemed that the average house without young children did not generate enough work to occupy four grown women full-time.

The vegetable garden had never been so well-tended. It wasn't enough, and she was in danger of growing bored.

Rhoda, who like Lida Mae did her own sort of quilt-inspired art in addition to the traditional fabric quilts they all made with their *maem* at the shop, wove baskets made to look like quilt blocks. They were very popular and sold almost as quickly as they were placed in the shop.

Some afternoons when they weren't working in the shop in Charm, they spent time together in their little home shop in an outbuilding they shared with their father. Each had his or her own area set up to suit their needs.

Lida Mae and Rhoda had just finished putting away the wash they'd hung out that morning, for it was a fine day. They'd decided to go out to the workshop and put time in on a couple of projects they wanted to take into the quilt shop to sell that week.

Lida Mae had barely sat down at her table when the door to the shop opened and her dad poked his head inside. "*Ach, gut*, there you are, Lida Mae. I need you to take Obadiah to visit Rebekah. Do you mind?"

She gave her current project, a set of mosaic glass-and-concrete coasters made to look like tiny log-cabin quilt blocks, a regretful look, then pushed back from the table. "Of course, I don't mind, *Dat*. And Rhoda and I made up a big batch of soup this morning. There's plenty for us and for Rebekah."

Rhoda stood up and set down her tools. "I'll go with you."

"Bebe Yoder is there with her. There might not be a lick of work for us to do, knowing how energetic that woman is," Lida Mae pointed out.

Rhoda shrugged. "Well then, at least we'll have offered. Come on."

Soon they were tooling down the road toward Rebekah's house, which was only about half a mile from their farm. Rhoda was driving, with Obadiah in the front passenger seat, and Lida Mae was in the back. The food was in the little trunk, accessed from the back.

When they reached Rebekah's house, an older woman from their church community, Bebe Yoder, stepped out onto the back porch, a dishtowel in her hands. She shaded her eyes, and when she recognized Rhoda, she smiled and waved the towel.

They hopped out, Obadiah climbing down more slowly, and retrieved the soup, bread and some fresh butter and milk from the back of the buggy, then headed to the house.

"Welcome! Oh, Rebekah will be very glad to see all of you." Bebe smiled coyly at Obadiah. "Maybe especially you, Obadiah. She's asked if you were coming twice already today!" She bustled back into the kitchen, followed by Obadiah and the two sisters, who were doing their best to hide amused smiles at Bebe's not-very-subtle matchmaking.

"You've brought food, how lovely! Ah! Vegetable soup and fresh bread and butter. She can have this tonight for dinner. Now, Obadiah, you just take this fresh *kaffi* I made. I've got two mugs right here! Go on in and visit. I've got everything set to rights, girls, nothing left for you to do in here. Perhaps you could weed her garden while she and Obadiah have a cozy visit? She's got herbs she's fretting about harvesting. I don't know a thing about them. But there are vegetables, too, that could use picking. I need to go home and get dinner ready for my Hiram, or I'd stay and help. But I'll be back in the morning. And later, Rebekah's son will be home from work. He's staying here nights for now, as he's unmarried and has bachelor's rooms in town, where he works."

She paused a moment and studied the sisters. "You know, he might do for one of you. He's handsome and has a *gut* job at the window factory. You could do worse!"

Looking at one another in alarm, Rhoda and Lida Mae

thanked Bebe for her interest in seeing them settled, but declined her kind offer. The older woman gave a puzzled smile, and said, "Okay, but if you change your mind, let me know. I do like helping *die youngie* find happiness together."

Bebe hurried to the door, then took her black bonnet from a peg and tied it under her chin over her prayer *kapp*. "Ah, here's my ride, right on time. I'll see you soon! *Denki* for bringing Obadiah over—he does cheer her up!"

Out the door she went, still chattering at them, and then at her husband, who was picking her up in an open pony cart. He grinned and waved at them, and then they headed down the driveway toward home.

"Goodness, you don't need to talk around Bebe!" Rhoda laughed as they went back inside.

"*Nee*. She takes care of both sides of a conversation. Imagine her trying to set us up with Rebekah's son. And calling us *youngie*! We're both beyond our teen years!"

"Maybe not to her eyes," Rhoda said. "It's all relative." She grinned when Lida Mae pulled a face. "Well, shall we say hello to Rebekah before getting to work?"

They walked into the living room, where Obadiah was already seated, drinking coffee with Rebekah.

"Girls! *Denki* for bringing Obadiah to visit." She took a sip of coffee and grimaced. "Decaf. Ugh."

"Doctor's orders, Rebekah," Obadiah reminded her mildly, drinking his own weak brew good-naturedly.

"*Ja, ja*, I know! And that tyrant Bebe won't let me lift a finger in my own house. Not even to wash the dishes or make my own bed!"

"Well, you're not supposed to do heavy housework, and no outside work yet," Rhoda pointed out. "But I'd think you could wash dishes. Wouldn't standing there be aerobic exercise of a sort?"

"Hmph! Try telling her that. I am supposed to go walking, but she doesn't know that it's a *gut* idea yet."

Obadiah frowned. "Where are your discharge papers?"

Rebekah picked up a thick sheaf of papers from the table next to her chair. "Here. You'll see for yourselves. It's like I'm a prisoner."

Lida Mae hid a smile behind her hand, but Rebekah caught her. "Oh, and what are you laughing at, missy?"

"It's just that you're normally the one ordering other people around when they've been sick."

Rebekah sat back, staring at Lida Mae, and the corner of her mouth lifted. "You're right. I'm being insufferable."

"Not insufferable, and your frustration is understandable," Rhoda assured their friend.

"It does say you should spend two and a half hours a week doing brisk aerobic exercise," Obadiah said thoughtfully. "Biking, swimming…ah! Walking." He looked up, over the top of his half readers. "Do you want to go walking every day?"

Rebekah perked up immediately. "*Ja!* I'd love that! But I'd have to go to town, maybe to the high school. I could walk on the track."

"I'll take you," Lida Mae said. "I could take you both, if you'd like to walk, too, Obadiah?"

He smiled and nodded. "*Ja!* It will be *gut* for us both. Can we start tomorrow?"

Rhoda and Lida Mae looked at each other. "Hmm. We're scheduled in the shop tomorrow afternoon. How would morning work?" Rhoda asked.

"Works for me, but you'll have to bust me out of here. Bebe won't like it," Rebekah predicted darkly.

"I'll convince her it's what the doctor ordered," Obadiah said. "*Gut!* So that's settled. We'll come for you at nine o'clock, *ja*?"

Rebekah nodded happily, and the girls asked about the gardening needs. After receiving instructions on what to harvest and how, they collected shears and baskets from the mudroom and headed outside.

"Well, the work won't do itself," Rhoda said, trotting down the three concrete steps to the yard and starting around back to where Rebekah's gardens were located.

Lida Mae followed her sister down the steps and was about to start around the house when she heard a buggy approaching.

"Now, who could that be?" Rhoda asked, peering toward the road.

"Go ahead and get started. I'll wait and see," Lida Mae offered. Rhoda nodded and continued around the large, white farmhouse. Shading her eyes, Lida Mae looked toward the road and was surprised to see Tom bowling along in his borrowed buggy with Toad, the big standardbred gelding *Dat* was letting him use, between the shafts.

"Nice timing," she murmured. "If Tom isn't busy doing something for *Dat*, I'll see if I can lasso him into helping us weed and harvest Rebekah's garden." Planting her hands on her hips, Lida Mae stood and waited to hear what Tom needed, a small smile playing about her lips as she anticipated roping the Texas cowboy into helping out with a little garden work.

Tom pulled up on Toad's reins and set the buggy's floor brake, then opened the door and climbed down. He'd seen Lida Mae's expression when he was pulling up to the hitching rail, and the mischievous gleam in her eyes had him wondering what she was up to.

"Hey, Lida Mae," he said. "Nice place. Isn't Rhoda with you?"

"*Ja*, in the back, weeding the garden. In fact, if you have nothing better to do, I thought you might enjoy a little getting-back-to-nature yourself!" She quirked an expectant eyebrow and Tom felt amused. He almost wished he did have time to stick around and help the sisters, but he was on an errand.

"Sorry, as truly tempting as all that sounds, I'm here as a messenger and then I need to get back."

She gave him a wry smile. "Can't blame me for trying. So what's the message that couldn't wait an hour or two until we got home?"

"Ah, right. Your *maem* called the barn phone. The buggy went into a deep pothole on the way to the shop, and a couple spokes broke in one wheel. You dad asked me to see if you and Rhoda would mind picking up your *maem* and Priscilla after you finish here?"

"Oh, that's not *gut*. So we're down a buggy until the wheel can be fixed?"

"I guess so. It shouldn't take more than a couple of days, though, ain't so?"

She pursed her lips. "*Ja*. But Rhoda and I just promised Obadiah and Rebekah that we'd take them into town to the high-school track every morning so they can walk together. Rebekah needs to for her heart rehab."

"I think it will work out," he said slowly. "I've got this buggy, and if I'm working on the farm, that leaves it for your use, and your *maem* and sister can take the other buggy that your *dat* usually uses to go into town to the shop."

Then, from around back, Rhoda called, "Lida Mae, are you coming?"

"I'll be right there!"

"I'll walk back there with you," Tom said, following her around back. He really did need to get back to the farm. But he figured a few more minutes wouldn't hurt anything.

"Wow, this is a really nice setup," Tom said, gazing at the extensive gardens that took up a good quarter of an acre behind the house.

"Took you long enough," Rhoda said, then her eyes traveled past her sister, and widened as she saw Tom. "Oh! Sorry, I didn't know you were here. I figured someone was here to see Rebekah. Is everything alright?"

He filled her in quickly on the buggy situation, then let his eyes travel across the yard. There was a large vegetable garden, another large herb garden and a small orchard toward the back of the yard.

"I like how she has brick paths through the herb and vegetable gardens," he commented, thinking his mom would really like this.

Then he stopped, and thought about how his *maem* was part of the reason he was in Ohio, and yet he still cared about what she would like and thought about how it could be done to please her.

"I guess that makes me a fool," he muttered.

Lida Mae, who was close enough to hear, turned and regarded him curiously. "What makes you a fool?"

"Um, nothing. Sorry."

Her eyes flashed, and she shrugged. "Sorry to intrude."

Great. Now I've gone and undone the progress we've been making on our...friendship? Association? Ach! Whatever we are. He sighed. "I was just thinking that my *maem* would like these brick paths and I wondered if we could do them in her gardens."

She looked puzzled. "That's nice. You're a *gut* son." She peered at him. "So...why didn't you want to tell me that? It reflects well on you."

"After what I told you last night you have to ask?"

She paused a moment and nodded. "Right. Well, I guess that you're just in the habit of doing nice things for the people you love. The fact that you and your parents currently disagree doesn't change the fact that you do love them, or your basic personality."

He shook his head. "Spoken like one who knows. You pretty much hit that nail on the head, Lida Mae. I should have told you my problems the day I met you. Maybe by now I'd be farther along the road to knowing what I'm going to do with my life." He gave her a crooked smile.

"Are you guys about done talking?" Rhoda commented from the garden. "It's getting sticky and hot. I want to get this done."

Lida Mae gave a start and turned to look at her sister. "Sorry, Rhoda! I got distracted. It's all Tom's fault." She gave him a little grin, and he smiled back, grateful that he hadn't alienated her after all.

"Sorry I can't stay and help. I'll see you both at dinner." He waved and walked around the house to where he'd left the buggy.

Lida Mae is right. Even though I'm upset with my parents, I love them. That's not going to change. He climbed into the rig and headed down the driveway, catching sight of the sisters working harmoniously in the garden as he turned onto the road.

Just like my brudders *and I have always worked. I miss them. But maybe I need to start accepting my new reality, and considering ways to make it work instead of spending all my time bashing my head against it like a ram trying to get out of a field.*

Another mile down the road, a thought occurred to Tom.

"I need to help Lida Mae get what she wants," he murmured, a rush of rightness washing over him. "I don't want to be the guy who showed up and stole somebody's life!" He drove on another mile, and the beautifully tended fields and pastures of the Beiler spread appeared ahead of him, making him even more certain of his sudden need to help the fiery redhead. Lida Mae, he knew, was partly responsible for the fitness of their farm and ranch. She deserved to continue doing what she loved.

"I need to help her figure out how to get her parents to let her resume her ranch and farm work, and make sure they don't try to stop her from creating her amazing glass art. Even if my *brudders* and I can't have what we want, I need to help her get what she wants. It's the right thing to do."

He thought he and Lida Mae were forging something that felt oddly like friendship, and he was determined to help his new friend.

"The only question is, how?" He grimaced as he considered that his powers of persuasion had so far failed to move his own parents in their decision. How did he think he could convince Lida Mae's parents to change theirs?

"There must be something I can do. I'll pray about it, and I'll talk to Lida Mae and see what she thinks."

He pulled up to the hitching post and saw Jackson striding out of the barn leading a two-year-old Belgian filly toward the exercise ring. He returned Jackson's wave and hopped down from the buggy, still watching Jackson and the filly—a horse of exceptional conformation and grace. He blinked—wasn't that one of the fillies Lida Mae had personally bred?

He shook his head, amazed that Jackson couldn't see for himself what a mistake he was making in removing his daughter's influence in running the ranch. She obviously knew horseflesh, and had helped significantly strengthen the Beiler lines of both Belgian and Haflinger horses. He'd seen the breeding books himself, and had been impressed with Lida Mae's insights and suggestions.

Why would any man want to push away someone in his own family who had knowledge and skills that helped make the family business stronger?

Then he gave a mirthless laugh, for his own parents had done exactly the same thing, hadn't they?

Tom unhitched the gelding from the buggy, and started for the barn to give the horse a good rubdown before beginning the afternoon chores. "Nevermind that. I'm thinking about Lida Mae's future now, not mine. And I think I might know a way to help her regain the future she wants."

A smile spread slowly over his face as an idea took shape. Now if he could just pull it off.

"How I'd love to be here to see Lida Mae's long-term success!"

Another thought took root in Tom's mind. What if he could stay to see Lida Mae shine? What if he gave up the idea of going home and stayed in Ohio, doing what he loved right here on the Beiler spread?

What if he and Lida Mae could have a future together?

He frowned. "What if she thinks I'm only interested in her because I can't have my own ranch, and thinks I want hers as a consolation prize?"

The irony of the situation did not escape him. "*Dat* and *Maem* said I should see if one of the Beiler *maedels* suited me. I refused to consider it at first because I was determined to go home." He winced when he remembered mentioning the girl he'd fancied back in Texas; a girl he'd never even asked out, who seemed colorless and boring when compared to Lida Mae's vivid energy and determination.

"I wish I could take that back," he muttered, continuing into the barn and caring for the horse before grabbing the wheelbarrow and pitchfork. "Maybe it's not too late. The more I get to know Lida Mae, the more I realize she suits me just fine. Now I have to figure out how to convince her that I'm exactly what she needs in a husband."

He started on the first stall in the long row. "That should be simple…not!"

Then he realized he was getting the buggy before the horse. "*Ach*, first I need to help her secure her place on her family ranch and farm in her own right. Then, once she's safe in her position here, I can think about convincing her that the only thing missing from her perfect future, is me."

Chapter Seven

For the next several days, the Beilers juggled buggies, and Jackson hauled out the little pony cart Lida Mae and her sisters sometimes drove, pulled by one of the Haflinger horses.

"I'd forgotten how much I enjoyed driving this little open cart!" Lida Mae grinned over at Priscilla as she steered the game little mare into town to relieve their *maem* and Rhoda at the shop. "It's fun!"

Priscilla laughed. "I know! And Sari is such a *gut* girl, aren't you, Sari?" she crooned to the mare, who perked up her ears as she trotted along. "*Denki* for picking me up."

"Sure! I knew you let *Maem* take your buggy since Danny is hanging out with her today."

"*Ja.* I really prefer that he ride in his booster seat, and it's easier to leave it strapped in my buggy."

Danny was Priscilla's five-year-old son. Lida Mae's oldest sister had lost her husband, Levi, several years earlier in a work-related accident. She and Danny lived a few miles away from her parents' spread on the farm she'd shared with her husband, which his younger brother, Menno Lapp, now farmed for her.

Lida Mae had been driving Obadiah and Rebekah to the high-school track in the mornings while it was cool.

With August upon them, the afternoons were typical of Ohio weather—hot and humid.

After dropping off Rebekah, she'd driven home with Obadiah, who had gone into the bunkhouse for lunch and some reading time. After her own quick lunch, she'd picked up her sister and the two women had driven to Charm.

She tied Sari up behind the quilt shop, gave her a feed bag and she and Priscilla grabbed their things. Before they could go inside, however, Priscilla caught Lida Mae's arm. "Wait a minute, Lida Mae. I want to ask you a question."

"*Ja?* What is it?"

A twinkle appeared in Priscilla's eyes. "I just wondered what's happening with you and Tom Fisher? Ever since you two stayed at the community center late after CPR class, you two seem to have reached some sort of, I don't know, accord, I guess."

Really, *really* not wanting to talk about the Texas cowboy, mostly because her feelings about him and the whole situation were now complicated by a growing liking for the man, Lida Mae shrugged. "I don't know what you mean, Prissy. Come on, *Maem* is probably ready to hand your adorable, but energetic son over to you."

She tried to take a step, but Priscilla's grip on her sleeve tightened. "Come on, Lida Mae. Spill. What happened between you two that night? Rhoda and I have both noticed you two are actually being nice to each other. Have you changed your mind about marrying him if he's the last Amish man in Ohio?"

Huffing out an exasperated breath, Lida Mae firmly removed her sister's hand from her arm. "If and when Tom Fisher is the last Amish man in Ohio, you can ask me again. For now, I'll just say he was really interested in my glass art. He asked intelligent questions and commissioned me to create a piece for his *maem*!"

Priscilla looked amused. "Ah! I see! The way to your heart is through your art!"

"Ha ha. We actually had a nice talk on the way home, and he explained more about his life to me." She frowned uncomfortably, unsure how much of what Tom had told her she could share. "He hasn't exactly had it easy recently, and I think that talking it out helped both of us. In fact, we have a lot in common. If you really want to know, I'm trying to think of a way I could help him out."

Priscilla's eyebrows rose skeptically. "So you no longer think he came here to steal your life?"

"I'm sorry I ever said that! It was childish. Look, I'll tell you more later. But for now, we need to get inside."

"Promise you'll fill me in?"

"As much as I feel I can, *ja*."

"Hey, sisters before misters!"

"Are we *kinner* again? Come on before *Maem* comes looking for us." She headed up the steps to the back door of the quilt shop, only to stop at her sister's next comment.

"You've seen how much he looks at you, right?"

Lida Mae turned to face her oldest sister, who had a smug smile on her face. "He does not."

"Oh, *ja*, he does! Whenever you aren't looking."

"Then how would I see him looking?"

"I think he likes you!"

Before Lida Mae could answer, the back door of the shop flew open, and a small voice cried out, "*Maem! Aenti* Lida Mae! You're finally here!"

"Danny!" Giving her son a hug, she smiled at Clara over his dark head. "Was my *lieb* a *gut* boy?"

"Of course, he was!" Clara answered as the sisters came inside and closed the door. "He almost always is."

"The number of cookies you feed him may be part of the reason for that, to be fair," Rhoda quipped from the table, where she was finishing her lunch.

"Have you had a lot of customers this morning?" Lida Mae asked.

"Ja!" Rhoda nodded. "There was a tour bus. Your last big stained-glass quilt block sold, as well as all the little suncatchers."

Lida Mae experienced the familiar pang of regret she always got when one of her lovely glass creations found a new home. This one had been a log-cabin block in shades of blue. But she reminded herself that she made them to sell. *"Ach*, that's *gut*! I'll use the money to get fabric for a new dress. I think I'd like a teal one."

Clara nodded. "You could use a couple new dresses to catch the eyes of the young men in the gmay. I'll give you the money for a second dress. Maybe pink?"

All Lida Mae could do was nod her thanks. She doubted a new dress was going to make up for her height and age, but supposed it couldn't hurt.

"Gut!" Clare continued. "Now, I've decided that I'll spend the afternoon here at the shop instead of going home. Priscilla needs to take Danny home for his nap. So you and Rhoda can go on back to the farm. Just remember to come back for me later."

"Are you sure?" Priscilla asked. "I don't mind staying. Danny can nap on the cot in the office if you need me."

"Nee, nee, go on. I'll be fine. Some of the girls from my quilting circle are coming, and we may start a new quilt." She rubbed her eyes. "Not a white-on-white!"

Before climbing into her buggy, Priscilla turned to

Lida Mae. "Do you mind watching Danny tomorrow afternoon? I've got an appointment in town. I figured I'd just stay all day, and I don't want him having to. He gets cranky after a few hours."

"Sure, he'll have fun with his favorite *aenti*," Lida Mae said.

"Hey!" Rhoda cried as she climbed into the pony cart with Lida Mae. "I thought I was his favorite *aenti*!"

As she drove home, Lida Mae couldn't help recall Priscilla's remark about how Tom supposedly watched her when she wasn't looking.

Not sure how I feel about that, she mused. *But it would be a lie to say I hate the thought. And whatever I am, I'm no liar. So, the Amish cowboy watches me? I'll have to see if I can catch him at it.* She grinned, feeling happy and carefree for the first time in weeks.

Tom shaded his eyes against the early afternoon sun and watched Lida Mae guide the little golden mare, no more than thirteen hands, up the driveway. She was smiling at something her sister, Rhoda, was telling her, and Tom thought she looked breathtakingly alive and vital. Ach! *There she is! Maybe I can finally get two minutes alone with her.*

He'd been trying, fruitlessly, to get Lida Mae alone so he could talk to her about his idea ever since he'd had it, days ago!

He glanced at Jackson, who was working with one of the two-year-old Belgians on a lunge line, putting her through her paces.

"Here comes Lida Mae, Jackson. Why don't I help her with that mare?"

Jackson barely glanced away from the spirited young

mare he was training, another of his daughter's fillies, and nodded. "Sure, go ahead. And maybe you could bring us back some lemonade when you're done." He wiped a big blue handkerchief across his forehead and blotted the back of his neck. "It's getting mighty hot out here in the sun!" Jackson returned his attention to the big two-year-old at the end of the lunge line.

Tom climbed the fence and dropped down to the other side, moving at a diagonal line across the yard to intercept the sisters as they pulled in at the barn. Striving for a casual tone, he greeted them.

"Hey, Lida Mae, hey, Rhoda."

Flashing Tom a shy smile, Lida Mae pulled up on Sari's reins, gently bringing the honey-colored mare with her lovely white mane and tail to a halt, and before she hopped down from the little one-seat pony cart. He moved up and began unhitching the mare from the cart.

"You know, I can do that," she said as Rhoda waved and headed toward the house, but he noticed the remark was delivered without her former heat.

"Of course, you could, but I was just standing around watching your *dat* lunge that filly, and I was feeling kind of useless. I don't mean to challenge your abilities, Lida Mae."

Those delicate red eyebrows arched toward her prayer *kapp*, and Lida Mae watched him with expressive green eyes.

He heaved a sigh and returned his attention to the small chore of unstrapping the mare's tack. "I just wish he'd let me actually do something important, you know?"

She snorted out a laugh, and Tom caught his breath at how the smile that followed lit up Lida Mae's face.

He found himself unable to look away. Lida Mae didn't seem to notice.

"*Ja*, when *Dat* gets in the groove, he's not real *gut* about sharing the work. Have you gotten your hands on any of the young stock yet? Or have you just been standing around 'watching and learning,' as *Dat* likes to say to justify hogging all the fun to himself?"

Tom couldn't help the bark of laughter that escaped him, because Lida Mae's rather impertinent description of "working" with her *dat* in the ring was right on target.

"Well, now you mention it, no, I haven't gotten to do any of the work," he admitted. "But I don't mind watching. Your *dat* sure knows his business."

Lida Mae shook her head in disgust. "Tom, you need to learn to assert yourself. If you don't, you'll never get to hold the end of that lunge rope."

She strode toward her father in the ring, and Tom, halfway through unhitching the mare, was helpless to stop whatever she had in mind.

"Lida Mae!" he called, trying not to be too loud so Jackson wouldn't hear him. "Wait! What are you doing? Oh, *sis yuscht*!"

Lida Mae had reached the ring and was leaning casually against the fence slats, watching her *dat* and the horse he was training. He glanced over and lifted his chin in acknowledgement. "Hey, Lida Mae. *Wie gets?* Where's Tom with my lemonade?"

"I'm *gut*, *Dat*. So, speaking of Tom, are you ever going to let him have a turn, or are you going to keep all the fun stuff for yourself and just use him as cheap farm labor?"

Jackson looked a bit surprised, then grinned. "Well, he's not that cheap—have you seen how much he eats?"

Tom, who had tied Sari to the hitching post, where she

was happily cropping grass, hurried up beside Lida Mae in time to hear her comment to her father and his reply. He groaned. "I'm fine with that, really," he protested, elbowing Lida Mae the way he would one of his brothers when they annoyed him.

Lida Mae grinned over at him. "Oh, be honest, Tom. You're dying to get your hands on this big girl, ain't so?"

"I...what?" At his shocked expression, Lida Mae burst out laughing. "The filly, Tom."

Understanding dawned, followed by a fierce blush, and Tom tried to deny it. "No, I..." Tom let his gaze move to the magnificent Belgian filly, who was still moving in a circle, now at a nice lope as Jackson turned in place in the center. "Well...*ja*, I have to admit I'd really like to work with her. She's a beauty, Jackson."

Jackson grinned over at the two young people. "Of course, she is! I bred her!"

Lida Mae cleared her throat. "Who bred her, *Dat*?"

Jackson cast a surprised glance at Lida Mae, and then back at the filly. "Oh! Well, you've got me there, Lida Mae. You did breed this particular filly, didn't you?"

Tom gave Lida Mae a respectful look. "You sure do *gut* work, Lida Mae. I've been looking through the breeding books in the office."

Blinking in surprise at the unexpected praise, Lida Mae said, "Well, *denki*, Tom. Matching mares and studs is a special area of interest for me."

"Now you've done it, Tom," Jackson said, throwing his daughter a fond look as he continued to work with the filly. "She's going to start talking bloodlines."

"*Dat!* Don't tease." Her face became enthusiastic as she said, "But I do know the bloodlines of every horse on this spread going back fifteen generations. I'm sure you're aware from your own family's American Quarter Horse breeding business that most breeders only track to ten."

Tom nodded, enjoying the way her eyes lit up when she talked about one of her passions. Then he looked at Jackson. "You're sure fortunate to have such a gifted equine matchmaker on your spread, Jackson. There are outfits back in Texas who pay a lot of money for someone with that kind of knowledge."

Lida Mae looked surprised, but Jackson chuckled and brought the trotting filly to a stop. "Sure, but I doubt any of them are women," he carelessly said, not seeing how his comment caused Lida Mae's face to fall. Before Tom could think of anything to say, she turned and stiffly walked away. "I'll just rub Sari down and put her out to pasture while you men get about your important work."

Tom and Jackson watched her go, Tom feeling dismayed at the sudden reversal of the situation, and Jackson looking a bit surprised, to Tom's mind.

"*Ach*, sorry, Tom, that was my fault. I seem to have a gift for putting my foot in it. But back to your job here; she's right, you do need hands-on experience. Climb in here and you can put her through her paces. Start by reversing her direction."

Tom stood where he was. "Jackson, why did you say that, about breeding operations not hiring women? You hurt Lida Mae's feelings."

Jackson shot a doubtful look after his retreating daughter, then looked back at Tom. "Do you think so? I didn't mean to. And anyway, she needs to hear the truth and give up her silly girlhood dreams if she's to become a wife and mother to an Amish man."

"What truth, Jackson? The fact is, plenty of women work on ranches and farms—*ja*, even Amish women—

where I come from. And I've seen women doing farm chores here in Ohio, too."

Jackson frowned. "Married women, maybe. But not young single Amish women. Maybe after Lida Mae finds a husband she can talk him into letting her work on his spread. But for now, she'll have to give up unrealistic ideas like that. Now, are you coming in here or not?"

With a last, regretful look at Lida Mae, who was vigorously brushing the Haflinger mare down before putting her out into the pasture, Tom hopped over the fence and hurried toward the big man and the bigger horse.

Once he had the filly turned and trotting in the opposite direction, he turned and looked at Lida Mae, still working with the little horse.

I'm sorry Lida Mae is out of sorts, but I'm grateful she spoke up and reminded her dat *that I'm here to work with the horses! And maybe by reminding Jackson how rare and valuable his daughter's horse sense and knowledge are, I've planted a seed that will take root, helping her in turn. Now, if I can just get her alone long enough to tell her about my plan to restore her to her former position here, I'll really be making progress!*

The filly nickered and tossed her head. "Tom, quit daydreaming and pay attention to that filly! She could hurt you or herself if she got out of control."

Jackson's reprimand snapped his full attention back to the horse. He'd figure out how to help Lida Mae later; for now, he was going to do what he'd been raised to do—work with horses—even if it was on an Ohio farm instead of on his family's Texas ranch.

Lida Mae brushed Sari with long, smooth strokes, removing dust and dirt from her golden coat and paying special attention to areas where tack touched her while she pulled the cart.

While she brushed she muttered to herself. Sari, munching on grass, ignored her. "Okay, *ja*, that hurt. But *Dat* didn't mean anything by that remark. To him, it's just fact. And for all I know, he's right." She sighed.

Running a hand down the horse's front leg, she encouraged the little mare to lift her foot, and used a hoof pick to dig out the few little pebbles she'd picked up on the road. Then she released that foot and moved on to the other three, balancing each foot on her thigh and resting her head against the mare's flank as she worked.

"Sari, you don't know what it's like. You're not considered delicate or fragile because you're female! You get to do what you were born for, pulling a cart. Of course, you can also have babies—working hard doesn't mean you can't also be female. Why can't they see it's the same for me?" She inhaled deeply of the sweet, sweaty horsey smell—a scent she adored—and stood up to replace the hoof pick into the little toolbox in the cart.

"Okay, girl, into the pasture with your buddies." She opened the gate and turned Sari into the pasture. The little mare trotted off to join the rest of the mixed Haflinger and Belgian herd, and Lida Mae closed and locked the gate carefully. She leaned back against the gate for a moment, watching her father and Tom work with the lovely filly. Pleasure filled her heart at the sight of the beautiful horse, a gorgeous reminder of *Gott's* creation.

I need to keep my mind on my goals. I may or may not get to work with horses again regularly. But at least Maem and Dat haven't forbidden me from working with stained glass, and that's a big blessing for which I must be grateful.

She started toward the house to help Rhoda prepare supper, thinking about Tom and the things he'd shared with her about his life, and his own disappointed dreams.

Finding the kitchen empty, she made a cup of tea and sat down at the table to think.

"Maybe the way for me to be content in my own situation is to stop focusing on myself," she said as she dug a cookie from the cookie jar. "To do that, I should focus on someone else."

Turning her gaze to the paddock, visible through the kitchen window, she watched Tom as he moved with an unconscious masculine grace to match the filly as she went through her paces for him.

"Now there's someone who could use my help. I wonder if I could find a way to help convince his parents that they should let him return home, and work their spread with his two brothers?"

She nibbled a thumbnail as she considered the problem. Part of her felt sorrow at the idea of the handsome young Texan leaving Ohio. She was starting to enjoy matching wits with him, and it was nice to have someone take a genuine interest in what mattered to her for a change.

"*Nee*, Lida Mae. He's not for you."

She frowned as she thought about ways she could help her new friend; for that is what he felt like to her since their time in her glass studio.

A sudden thought occurred to her, and she sat up straighter in her chair. "What if he were so valuable as a horse breeder that different outfits were competing to hire him? Then his *dat* would surely want him to come home, ain't so?"

It seemed like a good idea but how could she make it happen?

And did she even want to? The idea of Tom leaving didn't fill her with satisfaction as it would have a few weeks earlier. Instead, it filled her with something akin to sadness.

"Lida Mae! You can not get attached to this man. He's not staying. Get that through your head. He's. Not. Staying."

"Who's not staying?" Rhoda's question startled Lida Mae, and she nearly spilled her tea.

"What? Oh, nobody. Just thinking out loud. Let's get supper started."

Silently, Lida Mae told herself that she was okay with Tom leaving, and that it was only the friend she would be missing, not the man.

She dug another cookie out of the jar and popped it into her mouth whole as she set about prepping for supper, knowing that she could lie to herself, and even try to believe the lie.

But that didn't mean that in her secret heart of hearts she didn't recognize the truth.

Tom Fisher was growing on her; and not just in a safe, platonic way, but rather in a way that was probably going to leave her feeling his loss in that secret heart of hearts in a way that wouldn't quickly heal.

Ach, Lida Mae, what have you gone and done now? And is there any way to fix this?

One thing she knew; if she were to honestly attempt to help Tom return to his own home, she could forget about any possible future with him. Not that she thought a future with the handsome Texan was likely anyway. But she knew that a dainty Amish *maedel* waited for him back home, and there would be no place there for an Amish Amazon like herself.

Lida Mae chuckled sadly as she and Rhoda put supper on the stove. Knowing what she had to do and doing it with a glad heart were not necessarily the same thing, it seemed. But she'd found in life that sometimes if you told yourself you were fine, and pretended to everyone else you were fine, one day you woke up and found out you really were. She just hoped this would be one of those times.

After she and Rhoda finished dinner preparations, she told her sister she needed to write a couple of letters. She didn't share that the letters were to people she hoped would help her put her plan to send Tom back to Texas, not with his tail between his legs, but with his head held high, into motion.

Chapter Eight

Tongue clamped between her teeth, Lida Mae carefully made a curved cut in a piece of clear yellow glass, giving a pleased "ah!" when it came away clean. She set the small piece on a tray already filled with other carefully cut pieces in several colors. She needed to make about a dozen of the small suncatchers made to look like quilt blocks of various patterns for the family's shop, since the tourist bus the day before had depleted her inventory. She also needed to finish the set of coasters she'd been working on.

Danny, whom she was watching that afternoon, was happily occupied sitting on the floor with some toy trucks. Her good dog, Blue, was lying on the floor near the little boy, snoozing.

The workshop door opened and Blue lifted her head to see who was coming inside. When she saw that it was Jackson, she flopped back down and closed her eyes with a sigh. Tom stepped inside next, and looked around the workshop curiously.

Seeing Tom and her *dat* reminded Lida Mae of the two letters she'd mailed that morning to Amish farmers out west who were business connections of her *dat's*. Since she often handled his correspondence when it came to their horse breeding operation, she'd thought of the men when she was racking her brain for likely outfits not too far from Tom's home that might be interested in hiring one or two able, experienced men like Tom and his *brudder*, Jake.

The only hitch was that when she handled her *dat's* correspondence, she did it as Jackson Beiler, and he then signed the letters. The men didn't necessarily realize they were doing business with a young woman.

This time, she'd written the men without her *dat's* knowledge, and she'd forged his signature. She felt guilty about this but didn't see a way around it unless she enlisted her *dat's* help. The problem was that she didn't think he would go along with her plan, as it would both cost him his new employee and go against his agreement with Tom's father.

I'm going to have to confess this later. But it'll be worth it if it helps Tom get back closer to home, and the life he misses.

Lida Mae was pulled from her musings by her *dat's* booming voice.

"There you are, Lida Mae! And who might this likely-looking youngster be?"

"Grossdaddi!" Danny cried, scrambling to his feet and running to hug his grandfather, who picked him up and tossed him gently into the air. "It's me, Danny! Your grandson!" The little boy giggled wildly as his grandfather caught him and hugged him hard.

"Well, look who's here, Tom! My favorite grandson!"

"Silly *Grossdaddi*! I'm your only grandson!" Danny giggled.

"Watch the ceiling, *Dat*, it's pretty low," Lida Mae reminded her father as she pushed her safety goggles up onto her forehead, then grunted when they dislodged her prayer *kapp*. She pulled them off and set them on her workstation, patting the *kapp* back into place.

"Then maybe I should take this *buwe* outside and see if I can toss him high enough to grab me some cotton candy!"

Danny's eyes grew huge. "Cotton candy?"

"Sure! You see it up there all the time—the fluffy stuff in the sky."

"Grossdaddi," the child said, and giggled. "Those are clouds!"

Jackson looked crestfallen. "Clouds? You mean, there's no candy up there?"

Danny reached out and patted Jackson on the cheek. "I'll share my snack with you, *Grossdaddi*."

Jackson kissed the boy and set him back on the floor. "That's why you're my favorite grandson!"

Tom smiled at their antics, and Lida Mae shook her head. "What are you men up to?"

"I'm headed into town to pick up some supplies, and Tom is going to repair some tack in the barn. Looks like it could storm, so I'm taking old Grumpus. I'll see you all later."

Lida Mae frowned and looked out the window. It was pretty dark and slightly ominous-looking; not the least bit like cotton candy. "Careful, *Dat*. That looks like thunderstorm weather for sure and certain."

"That's why I'm taking Grumpus. Nothing startles him."

"Probably because he's stone-deaf," Tom said, gaining a nod of agreement from Lida Mae.

"Whatever the reason, he's the horse for today. I'll see you all at supper!" He left, and Lida Mae assumed Tom would follow, but the handsome, dark-eyed Texan stood just inside the door, looking around curiously.

"Are you working on more glass?"

"*Ja*, as you see."

He wandered closer and looked at a finished suncatcher lying on a tray. "Pretty. I'll bet people grab these right up. What quilt pattern is that?"

"Wild-goose chase," she said, looking at the small piece of glass art rather than at the man whose proximity was making her feel sort of itchy. She was sorely tempted to tell him about the letters she'd sent, but she wasn't sure how he would feel about her interference, so she kept her mouth closed and heartily wished he would go repair tack in the barn so she wouldn't blurt out the whole plan then and there. She decided to hurry him along. "Well, nice seeing you, Tom, but we've both got work to do, so…"

He laughed. "Okay, I'm going. But I'd like to talk to you later about something." He paused a moment as if he had more he'd like to say, but he looked at Danny, who was making truck noises on the floor, and apparently decided to wait. He opened the workshop door and glanced her way again. "Later, then, Lida Mae."

She nodded and he gave a small smile. "See you, Danny."

"Bye, Tom!" The boy waved a dump truck as Tom, with a final glance at Lida Mae, exited the building.

"I wonder what he wants to talk to me about." She glanced out the window toward the barn and noticed that it was starting to rain. Thunder rumbled, but she and Danny were safe and snug in the little workshop.

"I'll just be a few more minutes, and then we'll go back to the house. I just want to be sure the storm has passed before we head outside."

"Okay, Aenti Lida Mae," the boy agreed, zooming a bulldozer around in a circle in a way no real bulldozer had ever traveled.

Lida Mae focused on her work, forgetting all about Danny and the passing time until she had finished the piece she was working on. She put her tools down and placed her hands on the small of her back, stretching to work out the kinks caused by hunching over the worktable. "*Ach*, *vell*, I've made *gut* progress. That's six finished suncatchers including the ones I did last week. I can give them to *Maem* tonight and she can put them up for sale in the morning."

Pleased with her work, she began straightening her tools and cleaning up her workstation. "Almost done, Danny," she said. "You've been a very *gut* boy, letting me get some of this work done."

Turning to where her nephew was playing a few minutes before, she had to blink a couple of times to understand what her eyes were telling her.

Danny wasn't there. Neither was Blue. She looked around the small shop building, even peering under the workbenches, but boy and dog were nowhere to be seen.

Glancing at the window, she was surprised to see bright sunshine where just a moment ago there had been rain.

She checked the battery clock on the shop wall, and was shocked to see that she'd spent much more time than she'd realized working on her project. "*Ach!* No wonder Danny got bored. It's been nearly an hour since I told him I'd only be a few minutes!"

She moved to the door and threw it open. Outside everything was freshly washed and sparkling with water droplets. The air smelled deliciously of rain and soil. There was no sign of Danny.

"He must have gone to the house." She hurried to the house, trotting up the steps and throwing open the kitchen door. "Danny! Where are you! You need to wait for Auntie Lida Mae, and not go off on your own like this."

No piping little voice replied. And if Blue was in the house, she would respond to her mistress.

Lida Mae tamped down the first curling threads of fear, and walked through the house, searching every room. Her nephew was not there.

Running back outside, she turned in a circle, and called, "Daniel Lapp! Where are you? Come here this instant!"

There was no answer. "Blue! Come here, girl!" Still nothing. If Blue could hear her mistress, she would at least bark to let Lida Mae know where she was.

"The barn! Maybe he went to see the new kittens!" She turned toward the barn, and ran right into a solid form; two strong hands grasped her by the shoulders, momentarily holding her secure against a strong, masculine chest while she caught her balance.

Looking up, she saw that it was Tom whom she'd nearly run over in her haste to find her nephew.

"Sorry, Tom, I didn't see you. Please let me go. I have to check the barn for Danny!"

He released her and stepped back. "Sure, I just didn't want you to fall when you bounced off me," he joked, but she was already halfway to the barn and didn't answer.

She hurried inside and blinked to adjust her eyes to the dim light. "Danny?" She raced to the ladder leading up to the hayloft and climbed up swiftly.

"Now, where are those kittens?" Searching between rows of neatly stacked square bales of straw and hay, Lida Mae found the nest of kittens so young their eyes hadn't yet opened. Their mama, a sleek gray tabby, was curled around her babies, nursing them. She squinted up at Lida Mae, but, recognizing her, didn't protest her presence.

Tom arrived behind Lida Mae, and the cat hissed at him.

"Danny isn't here. Where could he be?"

"Okay, let's be calm. I take it your nephew has given you the slip. We'll find him. Where did you last see him?"

Lida Mae was already headed back to the ladder. Turning, she grasped the handles and felt for the top rung with her foot, and started down. "I was working on glass, and lost track of time. He must have left without me noticing. I'm a terrible aunt! Priscilla will kill me!"

Following her down the ladder and outside, Tom grasped her arm. She spun around to face him. "Let me go! I have to find Danny!"

He let go and held up both hands. "*Ja*, I know. I'm trying to help. Let's use logic. Whenever I couldn't find something as a boy, my *maem* would say 'look with your mind, not your eyes.' It often helped. So where else would a young boy want to go on a farm, if not inside, or to see kittens?"

Lida Mae's face scrunched up as she thought. Then her eyes grew wide. "Oh! There's a new foal in the mare's barn! He was just saying the other day that he wanted to visit it, but we didn't have time. Maybe he went looking for it on his own. Come on!"

But when they reached the stall there was no little boy there, only a Haflinger mare suckling her young baby.

"Oh, Tom, where can he be? What if something has happened to him?"

"He's here somewhere. And am I to understand your

Lab, Blue, is with him? If so, you know she'll protect him, right?"

At her tearful nod, he smiled encouragingly. "Let's go back outside and search the property."

Swiping angrily at her tears, she nodded. "*Ja*, okay. *Denki* for helping me, Tom."

He handed her a clean handkerchief from his pocket, and she wiped her eyes and blew her nose. She started to hand it back, but stuffed it into her apron pocket instead. "I'll wash that. Come on, we can't waste time."

The two of them searched the farm, looking in the various barns and outbuildings, and even in the buggy barn. No Danny.

"Let's go check the pastures," Tom suggested. "Little boys like looking at big horses, right? I turned the horses back out after the storm."

Lida Mae brightened. "*Ja!* Why didn't I think of that?"

Together they walked back to the pastures. The little boy wasn't in the field with the mares and older foals. And he wasn't with the geldings and mares without foals. "Where could he be?" she asked herself. Then a thought struck her. "Oh! The stud! He's fascinated with the Belgian stud, Simon. Come on!"

Without thinking, Lida Mae grabbed Tom's hand and pulled him along as she ran back past the barns, and around to the pasture where their Belgian stud, Simon, lived with his gelding companion, Boss, an elderly standard-bred retired from pulling buggies. Boss was enjoying a snooze in the sunshine, but Simon was under the huge old red oak tree in the center of the pasture. And there was Danny, standing in front of the huge animal, holding up an apple for the horse as if he was offering a treat to a dog. And speaking of dogs, Blue was sitting beside him, looking as if she approved of the whole adventure.

Lida Mae was filled with incredible relief. "*Ach*, thank *Gott*! There he is!" But she was talking to herself, because with an oath not often heard from Amish men, Tom was clamoring over the wood rail fence and into the pasture.

"Tom? What are you doing? Danny's fine."

Tom turned and regarded her with disbelief. "Are you nuts? That big brute will likely kill him! We have to get him away from there!" He turned and slowly approached the 2,000-pound animal, which was gently lipping the apple from the boy's hand. Lida Mae hurried to catch up with Tom, realizing he didn't know that Simon was hand-raised and quite gentle.

She grabbed Tom's sleeve. "Tom, wait. Simon is not going to hurt Danny."

Looking at her incredulously, he asked, "How do you know that?"

"Because I bred him and raised him from a foal. You wait here. You're too agitated to approach a strange horse, let alone a stallion."

Tom halted, studying the tableau, and muttered, "I sure hope you know what you're doing."

"It'll be fine, Tom." Lida Mae walked confidently to where the boy was now stroking the horse's velvety pink nose. "Here you are. Tom and I have been looking everywhere for you. You need to tell me if you want to come see the stud, *fashtay*, Danny?"

The boy turned his head and grinned at his aunt, not realizing he'd made her frantic with worry. "Auntie Lida Mae! Look! I gave Simon an apple I found when I walked through the orchard. He likes it! He likes me!"

"Of course, he does, *lieb*. But you worried me, wandering off from the shop like that without a word. You know you shouldn't do that."

He looked up at his aunt, big, brown eyes filling with tears. "I'm sorry Aenti. I didn't mean to worry you. Blue was with me." Glancing over at Tom, who was slowly approaching, he looked stricken. "Did I worry Tom, too? I'm sorry!"

Lida Mae reached out and rubbed the big horse, who was lipping at Danny's little straw hat, on his long, bony nose, brown with a white star on the forehead. "That's not food, Simon," she said, scratching the stallion under his bristly chin right where he liked it. The horse closed his eyes in enjoyment and let out a protesting whicker when Lida Mae stopped her ministrations. "That's enough from you, big boy," she murmured. "I need to get this little boy back to the house."

"I'm tired," Danny complained. "I walked a long way to see Simon."

"I'll carry you if you like," Tom said, and waited to see if the boy, who was old enough to have some masculine pride, would allow it.

After a moment, Danny nodded. "Okay, *denki*, Tom." He held up his arms, and Lida Mae watched the strong young man swing the child into his arms, then up onto his shoulders. Danny squealed and Lida Mae grinned.

"Now, you can see the whole world!" she laughed, giving the horse one last scratch before turning to lead the way to the gate.

"I can!" Danny yelled from his perch atop Tom's shoulders. "I can see the driveway! *Maem* isn't back yet."

"Thank *Gott* for small favors," Lida Mae muttered, gaining a sympathetic grin from Tom.

They were nearly at the pasture gate when a loud

whinny sounded from behind them, followed by a thundering of hooves. Turning, Lida Mae was astonished to see Simon bearing down on them, nostrils flaring, fire in his normally placid eyes. Blue started barking wildly, and put herself between the oncoming horse and her people, continuing to bark at the huge animal bearing down on them as if she could turn him away with sheer determination.

"What on earth?" Lida Mae cried. The big horse cut off their path to the gate, and, tossing his head and whinnying loudly, herded them back away from the fence, the dog dancing and barking savagely. The horse paid her no mind.

Tom slowly handed a frightened Danny to Lida Mae and stepped between them and the angry horse. "He looks ready to kill something!"

"This isn't like him! I don't know why he's acting this way!" Lida Mae looked around, searching for a way out. "We'll have to go over the fence if he won't let us through the gate!" She started for the fence, but the horse once again got between her and escape, forcing the three humans back toward the center of the pasture. The dog circled around the horse, nipping at his heels, and was ignored for her efforts.

"Aenti Lida Mae? Is Simon gonna hurt us?"

"No, *lieb*. Simon wouldn't hurt us. I don't know what's gotten into him, but we'll be okay."

"Right, stay calm," Tom said, looking around.

"What are you looking for?" Lida Mae asked, keeping an eye on the horse, who seemed satisfied that they had moved far enough from the gate to suit him and had turned back toward the exit.

"I'm looking for a stick or a rock—something I could use as a weapon if I have to," Tom said.

"I don't understand. This isn't like Simon," Lida Mae muttered.

As if to prove her wrong, Simon reared up onto his hind legs, screaming a challenge as if at a rival stallion; except the only other horse in the paddock was old Boss, and he was standing across the space, watching the excitement from a safe distance.

"Get back!" Tom yelled, pushing Lida Mae and Danny farther from the horse. But Simon wasn't paying them any attention. He was charging forward at an unseen enemy, screaming a challenge. He reached the gate, and began rearing up and stomping the ground with his powerful front feet. He did this several times while the three humans watched in alarm, and the dog stood in front of them, hackles bristling, whining nervously. Had the big horse gone insane?

Just as suddenly as he had become violent, Simon calmed, dropping back down onto four feet and nosing something on the ground. Then he turned, blew air at them and walked quietly back toward his pal, Boss. Soon he was cropping grass as if nothing had happened. Blue walked stiff-legged toward whatever the horse had been stomping on, sniffed it for a few moments, then trotted over to touch noses with the horses, who acted as if everything was normal.

Lida Mae wasn't sure if it was safe to move. Would Simon attack again if they tried to leave the pasture?

Tom turned and looked at her, eyebrows raised. "I do not know what that was all about. But I suggest we leave while we can."

Agreeing wholeheartedly, she let Tom pluck Danny from her arms and start quietly back toward the gate.

"If he seems aggressive, run for the gate," Tom said. Lida Mae nodded, but the horse ignored them as they approached the gate. "What was he stomping on? It should be right about here."

Eyes scanning the ground, Lida Mae was about to step forward to unlatch it when she suddenly saw what had alarmed the horse. She jumped back with a small scream.

"What? What?" Tom cried, pulling her back against him and peering around her in alarm, one arm securing the child on his hip, the other banded protectively around Lida Mae's waist.

"Look! That's what made Simon behave so violently!"

All three of them stared at what was left of a snake lying in the path to the gate. Although the horse had made short work of it, its penny-bright head, very close in color to Lida Mae's hair, was still visible, identifying it as a mature copperhead.

Lida Mae and Tom looked at one another in disbelief. "The horse knew the snake was there, and wouldn't let us come this way so we wouldn't step on it," Tom gasped. "We might not have seen it in the grass!"

"Simon saved our lives!" Lida Mae whispered, looking at the dead snake.

"Well, probably not. Copperheads aren't usually deadly for adult humans. But if it had bitten Danny, that could have been dicey."

"Yuck. Well, I've got nothing against snakes, but when we find copperheads we usually relocate them to a wild area. We don't want them on the farm," Lida Mae said. "Come on, let's get back to the house."

She opened the gate, relatching it securely after they passed through.

Back at the house, she climbed the steps to the kitchen and held the door open for Tom.

"Come on, Tom. Let's get Danny inside. We could all use a cold drink and a snack after that."

A few minutes later, they were all seated at the kitchen table enjoying a snack. Lida Mae poured cold lemonade for everyone and sliced some cheese and apples. There was still no sign of the rest of her family.

Danny ate his snack quickly and asked to be excused to play with his farm set. Tom watched the boy dart into the living room, and soon heard him talking to the toys and setting up a little farm.

"He's a tough little guy. Resilient. Your sister must be proud of him."

Lida Mae sipped her coffee and nodded. "*Denki*. He is. His *dat* would be proud of him, too."

Tom watched her for a moment, wondering whether she would elaborate on what had happened to the boy's father. So far, nobody had explained it to him. As if sensing his regard, Lida Mae turned and returned his stare. "What?"

A bit embarrassed at the idea of prying, Tom did so, anyway. "I just wondered what had happened to Danny's *dat*. It's okay if you don't want to talk about it."

A look of sadness settled on Lida Mae's face. "Ah. Levi fell off the roof of a house he was working on about three years ago. He wasn't wearing his safety harness."

Tom half wished he hadn't asked. "*Ach*, no. That's too bad."

She nodded in agreement and sipped her lemonade.

They sat in silence for a few moments, then Lida Mae took a deep breath and looked Tom in the eye. "Tom, I need to tell you about something I did. I probably should have asked you first, but I needed to get it done before I lost my nerve."

She nibbled a thumbnail nervously and he wondered what she'd done, and felt a stirring of trepidation at her grim expression. "Well this sounds serious. I may need some strong, black *kaffi* to get through it, whatever it is."

As he had hoped, his attempt at humor lightened the mood. She cracked a smile. "You know, you drink an awful lot of *kaffi*."

"Hasn't hurt me yet. Although from your higher vantage point, you might think it's stunted my growth."

She laughed aloud and shook her head. "*Ach*, Tom! There's nothing stunted about you. I'll make *kaffi*, and then we'll talk, okay?"

He felt genuine warmth for this unusual, lovely, compassionate woman wash over him, and he smiled at her. "Agreed."

As Lida Mae bustled about making the hot beverage, Tom wondered what she had done that she should have cleared with him first.

He frowned, reflecting that he had a confession of his own to relate to Lida Mae. And he wasn't certain he was ready to do so yet. So he'd see what she had to say, and hope whatever it was wouldn't mess up the plans he'd started to put into place on her behalf.

Plans he knew could actually go either way, cementing Lida Mae's position on her family horse ranch and farm, where Tom now realized he hoped to stay, or changing the direction of her future in ways that might forever place her out of Tom's reach, ending his budding hopes that the two of them might have a future together forever.

In his heart, he knew he had to take the risk.

Chapter Nine

Lida Mae set mugs of hot, fresh kaffi on the table and sat. "I'm not sure where to begin."

Tom raised his eyebrows at that. "You've definitely caught my attention with your cryptic remarks."

She took a sip of kaffi and gathered her thoughts. How best to tell Tom what she'd done? What if he was angry instead of pleased? Well, Lida Mae, you should have thought of that before you mailed those letters! Since you didn't, there's nothing to do but fess up.

"Over the last couple weeks I've come to understand that no good will come from banging my head against the reality of my situation. I've been praying for *Gott* to help me accept my parents' decision, and to learn to enjoy, for now at least, being a 'proper Amish woman.'"

He didn't miss that little caveat. "For now?"

She shrugged, and a mischievous little grin appeared. "Sure. In time I may be blessed with a husband who actually appreciates my skills in horse breeding and training, and farm and ranch husbandry, and will welcome me working by his side."

"In Texas you'd have an easier time. I tried telling your *dat* that Texas women work alongside their men on the farms. Amish women, not just *Englischers*."

"But I'm guessing he wasn't buying that?"

Tom looked embarrassed. "Um, I think the real crux of the matter is that he's giving in to your *maem's* demands on this, right?"

"Exactly." She shrugged. "Not that it matters. I'll never find a man who can see past my height, let alone worry about what I'm capable of doing on a farm."

Tom took her hand, his earnest gaze meeting hers. "Look, Lida Mae, for what it's worth coming from a guy whose opinion may or may not matter to you, you're dead wrong about your appearance."

She just blinked at him, so he went on. "You're a very beautiful woman. Tall, graceful, strong, with perfect skin and that red hair! And those amazing green eyes! I think the real problem with the men around here is probably not your physical appearance, but rather your strong sense of your own worth, and your multitude of skills and talents."

She sat very still, her hand caught in his gentle grasp. "What are you saying?" she whispered, wide-eyed.

"Isn't it obvious? The men around here are scared to death of you. And since you took it the wrong way and assumed they didn't find you attractive, you only became more independent and more skilled, which frightened the young fools even more. What you should do is move to Texas. You'd find a *gut* man there fast enough."

Open-mouthed with amazement, Lida Mae just looked at him.

"Cat got your tongue?"

Lida Mae shook her head in wonder. "You think I'm beautiful. And you think the men around here are intimidated by me."

He just nodded. She sat back and considered the possibility. Tom released her hand and poured himself another cup of *kaffi*, waiting for her to speak.

"Huh. Okay, so assuming you're right, what do I do?"

He laughed and pointed at her. "That right there is the million-dollar question, isn't it? What do you do about your problems, and what do I do about mine?"

Lida Mae couldn't believe what Tom had said. He thought she was beautiful! And smart, and talented! She knew such things weren't supposed to mean a lot compared to what sort of character she had, and what her relationship with *Gott* was. But she couldn't deny they surely did. If a smart, handsome man like Tom thought such good things about her, could they be true? Could he be right? Were the men around here just ninnies? If she had the courage to leave, could she find a *gut* man elsewhere? Someone who would love her as she was, not try to form her into who he wanted or needed or thought she should be?

"I wish there was some way we could change our situations," he mused aloud, interrupting her thoughts. She stared at him, and realized he'd given her the perfect opening for her little confession. And there was no time like the present to get it out of the way.

"As to that, why couldn't we?"

He cocked his head questioningly. "Really?"

She nodded. "*Ja*. In fact, what I need to tell you relates to that very idea."

"Go on."

She sent up a quick prayer for courage and dove in. "I pray you won't be angry. But this morning, I mailed two letters to contacts of my *dat's* in the horse world. I'm sorry if I overstepped, Tom, but the realization came to me that just because I'm stuck here unable to do what

I love doesn't mean you should be!" She looked at him, trying to see how he felt, but his face gave away nothing about his thoughts, so she plowed on.

"These two men have big spreads out west. One is in Oklahoma and the other is in New Mexico. They're both *gut* men. I know because I handle most of my *dat's* correspondence, so I've dealt with them for years. They are both fair and honorable."

He blinked at her. "You wrote these men on…my behalf?"

She nodded. "*Ja*, on yours and your younger *brudder*, Jake's."

"To be certain I understand, you wrote them asking them to hire us? So we could get good jobs not too far away from where we grew up?"

She nodded. "I'm sorry, we don't have any connections in Texas except for…"

"Except for my parents?"

She nodded again, wishing desperately she could tell what he thought of the idea.

His eyes widened and he leaned forward. "Lida Mae, does your *dat* know about this?"

She felt heat wash over her cheeks and shook her head. *"Nee."*

"So these men will be comfortable dealing with you?"

She squirmed a bit in her seat before meeting his eyes. "They don't actually know it's me they'll be dealing with, is the thing."

He looked puzzled a moment, then his eyebrows shot up toward his hairline. "Are you saying that you wrote to these men as your *dat*? You forged his signature?"

Sure he was scandalized by her boldness and dishonesty, she nodded miserably. "You're right, Tom. I shouldn't have done it. Oh, *sis yuscht*! I'm going to be in so much trouble!"

Tom just stared at her for another few moments before throwing his head back and bursting into laughter.

Lida Mae's jaw dropped. "Why are you laughing? I know what I did was wrong and not my best idea, maybe, but I just told you I'm going to be in trouble and you start laughing? That's not very nice."

He held up a hand and tried to get himself under control. "I'm sorry, Lida Mae! Give me a moment." He took a couple of deep breaths before grinning at her.

"I wasn't laughing at you at all, please believe me."

"You could have fooled me." She folded her arms across her chest and glared at him, feeling like a fool.

"I'm really sorry, Lida Mae. Honest, I'm laughing because you took me by surprise with your sweet gesture. I don't know when anyone has ever gone out on a limb for me like that before. If ever."

"So, you're not mad at me?"

"Mad? When you've tried to help my *brudder* and me? No, of course not!"

"Oh. Then why are you laughing?"

He shook his head. "You won't believe me if I tell you."

"Try me."

"Okay, but I hope you aren't the one who's mad when you hear what I've done!"

Curious, she was about to ask what he meant when the sound of buggy wheels approaching along the driveway interrupted them.

"Hold that thought, Tom Fisher! You're not getting off the hook this easily!"

* * *

Lida Mae jumped up and opened the kitchen door to see who was coming, and exclaimed in surprise.

"It's the bishop's buggy! I wonder what he needs?"

Tom was disappointed that their discussion had been cut short right when they were actually getting somewhere. He was dying to learn more about the ranch operations out west Lida Mae had written to on his and Jake's behalf. How courageous of her! It was unfortunate that she'd done so without her father's approval, but he didn't exactly think he was in a position to judge.

What will she think when I tell her what I've done? I can only hope she'll be okay with it. I'm not sure how I feel about her writing to ranch owners for me—but her heart was in the right place, and who knows? If she isn't starting to have the same ideas about a possible future with me that I'm having about her, then I won't want to stick around here anyway. Oklahoma or New Mexico might be a perfect solution for Jake and me.

Lida Mae welcomed Ben Lapp and his wife, Sally into the house. A look at their faces caused Tom to forget all about his problems. Their expressions told him something was wrong.

"Ben, Sally," Lida Mae said. "Please come in and have a seat. We have fresh *kaffi* and some cheese and apples. Or there are cookies from this morning."

The Lapps murmured their thanks and came inside, hanging hat and bonnet on hooks inside the door and moving to the table to have a seat.

After pouring *kaffi*, Lida Mae sat down and looked at them both. "Alright, what's happened? Is it bad?"

Sally Lapp looked at her husband, who nodded at her, and she reached a hand across the table and laid it atop

Lida Mae's. "It's not awful, but it's not *gut*, either," the older woman said. "Your *dat* has been in an accident. His buggy was hit by a car that didn't see him in the storm. Fortunately, the driver must have glimpsed him at the last second, as she veered away, but not before clipping the wheel and causing the buggy to go out of control. It broke free of the horse and rolled into a ditch."

Lida Mae's hands came up and covered her mouth. "Oh, no! And *Dat*? Is he hurt?"

The bishop answered this time. "*Ja*, he's got a couple broken bones and a mild concussion. But he's going to be fine, according to the doctors at the hospital. Your *maem* and sisters are there with him now. They asked us to come here and tell you what was happening, since they knew they'd be late getting home."

Lida Mae jumped to her feet and looked around wildly. "I have to go to him! Oh, but I have Danny here, I can't leave." She looked toward the living room, and saw the boy standing in the doorway, silently listening to the adults speak. Lida Mae held out her arms, and he hurried to her.

"Is *Grossdaddi* hurt, Auntie Lida Mae?"

She hugged the boy and nodded against his shoulder. "*Ja, lieb*. But Ben said he's not too bad."

"Will he die?"

Ben reached out and patted the child on the shoulder. "Not today, Danny."

"My *dat* died."

Lida Mae sniffed back a sob, and Sally smiled at the child. "*Ja*, we know, *lieb*. He's with *Gott* now."

Danny nodded at this, and, having made certain that his *grossdaddi* wouldn't be joining his father in Heaven anytime soon, went back to the living room to play with his toys.

"I really want to see my *dat*, make sure for myself he's okay," Lida Mae whispered.

Sally nodded. "We figured as much. Mrs. Jones is on the way to fetch you. She'll be here soon. Why don't you gather what you need, and then you'll be ready when she gets here?"

"But Danny…"

"I'll stay and watch Danny. Well, Ben and I will." She smiled at her husband. "We've got a bit of experience raising *kinner*, you know."

Lida Mae nodded gratefully. The bishop and his wife had raised eight children, the youngest of whom was in his late teens. *"Denki."*

"Do you want me to go with you?" Tom asked a bit awkwardly.

"Nee, denki. Maybe you could do the evening chores. I'll be back in a couple hours."

He nodded, relieved there was something he could do to help. "Okay, then, I'll see you all later."

She nodded absently. "Oh! What about dinner?"

Sally waved a hand. "Ben went ahead and ordered pizza and salad to be delivered."

"And pop!" Ben added with a twinkle in his eyes.

His wife rolled her own eyes. *"Ja,* and pop. It's the perfect meal when you don't know when you'll get to eat, or how many people you'll need to feed. Don't worry. Just go."

Lida Mae gave Sally an impulsive hug, then hurried upstairs to get ready to go to the hospital.

Tom waited in the kitchen with Sally while Bishop Ben went into the living room with Danny to play with the farm set. When Lida Mae came back downstairs, Tom handed her a paper plate with a couple slices of pizza on it, and a can of soda, and told her not to worry about a thing, that he, Sally and Ben had things under control, and they'd see her later when she could bring them news of how Jackson was doing. A horn sounded from outside and Sally peered through the window.

"Your ride is here! Tell Jackson we're praying for him."

Tom opened the door and held the food while Lida Mae put on her bonnet. He accompanied her outside to the waiting car, and after she'd climbed into the front seat beside Mrs. Jones, who often drove her Amish neighbors around the area, handed her the pizza and pop. "I hope Jackson is okay," he said. "Let me know if there's anything I can do." He closed the door and watched the big van pull away, taking Lida Mae to Pomerene Hospital in nearby Millersburg. And as he headed to the barn to do the chores, he prayed that Lida Mae's father would soon be able to return home where he belonged.

Chapter Ten

Mrs. Jones pulled her van up to the front entrance of Pomerene Hospital in Millersburg, put it into Park, then turned to look at Lida Mae, who already had the passenger door open.

"Whoa, missy, hold on there. Tell your *maem* that I'll be back in an hour."

Lida Mae felt a surge of disappointment. "An hour? But that's hardly any time to visit!"

"I know, and I'm sorry, but I have another commitment tonight, and I'll need to pick you all up and get you back home in time to make it. One hour. I can bring you back tomorrow."

Lida Mae nodded reluctantly, and glanced at the clock on the van's dashboard. "See you at around six then."

Inside, she asked the elderly *Englisch* man at the reception desk for directions to her father's room.

She hurried down the hall to the elevators, arriving in time to follow three *Englisch* teens into a car. They were talking among themselves and paid her no mind.

"But are you sure Mom's okay?" a worried-looking young girl Lida Mae guessed to be around fifteen asked her two companions, a boy and a girl she took to be her siblings.

The girl, whom Lida Mae figured was a year or two older than the one who'd asked the question, reached out and took her sister's hand. "Dad said she was fine. Just the slight concussion from where she hit her head when the car spun and she hit the tree."

The younger girl's eyes filled with tears, and she blinked rapidly to clear them. Lida Mae didn't mean to eavesdrop, but they were talking right in front of her as if she didn't exist, so she couldn't really help it.

"I'm just glad she's okay," the boy, who looked to be the youngest of the three, said. "She could have been killed!"

The elevator stopped and the doors whooshed open, and the oldest girl, looking at the floor readout, said, "This is us."

As they exited, the first girl said, "I'm just so relieved Mom was able to swerve away from the buggy! If she'd done more than clipped it, she would have killed everyone inside and probably the horse. She wouldn't have been able to live with that."

Lida Mae's jaw dropped in surprise. As the doors slid closed, the oldest sister said, "God kept them all safe. Come on, it's this way."

"Their *maem* is the one who hit *Dat's* buggy!" She only had a few moments to reflect on the crazy circumstance of them all being on the same elevator before the doors again opened, this time on her floor.

In a bit of a daze, she stepped off the elevator, pondering the fact that the woman who had almost killed her father had just been made human to her through the unlikely circumstance of their children sharing an elevator.

"May I help you, dear?"

Lida Mae snapped out of her reverie and blinked at

the woman who had asked the question, a comfortably round Black woman in pink scrubs seated behind a desk opposite the elevator.

"Um, I'm looking for Jackson Beiler's room? I'm his daughter."

"Ah, yes, I could have guessed from your obvious resemblance to him! Come on, I'll show you the way."

"I don't want to trouble you…"

"No trouble. If I don't get up and walk around every so often, I get stiff. You're doing me a favor." She picked up a chart from the desk and led the way.

Before they reached the room, the woman slowed. "Listen, er, sorry, what's your name, sweetie?"

"It's Lida Mae."

The woman nodded. "Okay, Lida Mae. Your father is a very blessed man. He's still alive. But he has some bruises and some gashes that had to be stitched. He looks a bit… alarming. But he's going to be just fine."

Lida Mae took a deep breath, then let it out slowly and nodded. "*Denki* for the warning."

"Sure. I'm the RN on duty this evening. My name is Julie. Let me know if you or your family need anything." She waited for Lida Mae's nod, then turned briskly on the heels of her pink Crocks and entered a room a few feet down the hall. Lida Mae followed cautiously, wondering what she would see inside.

"Mr. Beiler, there's someone here to see you. And I'll just check your vitals while I'm here."

"My vitals are the same as they were an hour ago," Jackson grumbled, filling Lida Mae with relief. If her *dat* sounded that irritated, he must be alright. She stepped fully into the room, and saw her mother and her two sisters seated in chairs. They were watching as the nurse checked Jackson's blood pressure.

"Ouch! That thing is too tight! Are you trying to pop my arm right off at the elbow?"

Lida Mae smiled tremulously and shook her head. "What a relief," she said. "I can tell from your voice that you're going to be fine."

"Lida Mae!" Her *maem* and sisters all stood, taking turns hugging her, a few telltale sniffles escaping them unnoticed.

"Hey, who was in a buggy accident? Me! How come I'm not getting any hugs and kisses?"

Nurse Julie finished Jackson's vitals and noted the last of the data on his chart. She took a small paper cup from her pocket, and handed it to Jackson. "Here are your evening meds, Mr. Beiler. Take them with that water, please." He picked up a large plastic cup of water with a straw and took the pills. Nurse Julie nodded in approval and made a notation on the chart. "Good. Those will help with the pain, and prevent infection. You'll get more in a few hours. Let me know if the pain in your wrist, or your headache, get too bad before then."

"When can I leave?"

"The doctor is keeping you overnight for observation. You'll probably be discharged tomorrow morning."

"Tomorrow?" He pushed himself up one-armed into a sitting position on the bed. "I don't want to stay here! I want my own bed. How's a man supposed to recover if he has to sleep in a strange bed all alone?"

Lida Mae looked at her father, who had a bandage on his head rather than the usual straw hat. He had two black eyes and a stitched cut on his jaw. And one of his arms was in a sling, a cast on his wrist and hand. She winced.

He wouldn't like not being able to use that arm, no matter how fast it healed.

"*Dat*, did you break your arm?" she asked.

"*Nee*, it's just the tiniest hairline fracture," he said, casting a quick look at the nurse, who smiled and shook her head.

"It's a broken wrist, Mr. Beiler. We talked about this. You'll need to rest that arm and not use it for anything strenuous for a few weeks, until the doctor says the cast can come off. If you cheat, you'll exacerbate the injury and set yourself back even longer."

A mutinous expression Lida Mae knew well crossed her father's face, and he glared at the nurse. "But how can I work with my horses with a broken wrist?"

"You'll have to find someone to help with that. Now, I have other patients to check on. I'll see you later." With a smile at them all, she strode out of the room, chart under her arm.

They were all silent for a few moments while Jackson chewed over the fact that he was out of commission for an unknown time. Clara cleared her throat and said, "I'm sure Tom can handle whatever needs to be done—under your supervision, of course." Then, glancing at Lida Mae, she added, "And Lida Mae can pitch in where needed."

Lida Mae looked at her mother in surprise. She was to be allowed to work with the horses again? A feeling of happiness stole over her, despite her worry about her father.

"*Ja, Dat*, I'll do whatever you need, don't worry." Looking at her mother, she said, "And, *Maem*, I'll keep up with all the housework and do my part at the quilt shop, too."

Her mother patted Lida Mae's shoulder. "I know you will, *lieb*."

"We'll help out more in the house to free Lida Mae up," Rhoda said.

Priscilla nodded in agreement. "For sure and certain, *Maem*."

"There, you see?" Clara said reassuringly to her husband, whose pride had been injured along with his wrist and head. "Your family is behind you, Jackson. We'll get through this together, with *Gott's* help."

He slowly nodded. "*Ja*, I suppose we will."

They spoke of other things for a bit, catching each other up on their days, until Lida Mae remembered that Mrs. Jones would be back with the van soon. "Oh! It's almost time for our ride to get here! She has somewhere to be, so she only gave me an hour."

Clara pushed to her feet. "That's alright. We've been here for hours." She kissed Jackson on his forehead and smoothed his hair gently. "I'll be back in the morning, *lieb*. Try to rest well, and don't frighten the nurses with your grumpiness, *ja*?"

A sheepish look crossed his face and he smiled weakly. "*Ja*, okay. These medications are making me sleepy, anyway. Don't be late in the morning, though. I'll be ready to get out of here!"

"*Ja*, I'll see you as soon as I can get a ride after breakfast. Come, girls. Let's let your father rest."

The elevator arrived almost immediately, and Lida Mae recalled that she'd ridden up with the family of the woman who had caused the accident. She shared this with her family as they rode down to the first floor, and they all wondered at the strangeness of the timing.

"To me it's another example of *Gott's* goodness, girls,"

Clara said, wiping telltale moisture from her own eyes. "You were given a glimpse into their pain, Lida Mae. It makes them human to you. The woman who hit your *dat* is just human, too. And she's one of *Gott's* children, like all of us. They may worship differently, and dress and live differently, but in the end they're our brothers and sisters in Christ. I think *Gott* put you in that elevator with them so you could witness that for yourself."

"And the weather was probably mostly to blame," Priscilla added. "It would be hard to see anything in that driving rain, let alone a black buggy with a couple of flashing lights. She may not have been driving recklessly at all."

"We'll pray for her and her family," Clara said. "It will help us, too, to give forgiveness."

Her daughters nodded their agreement.

"When we get home, I'll get dinner on the stove, girls. Lida Mae, you see if Tom needs help with the chores. We'll eat as soon as everything is done, *ja*?"

"Okay, *Maem*," Lida Mae said, wondering if her gladness at being granted permission to do the work she loved due to her father's unfortunate accident and injury made her wicked. Then she remembered that dinner was already there, and told the others about the pizza dinner provided by the Lapps. At their glad exclamations, she realized it was okay to take bits of happiness where one could, even in dark times. It was a human thing to do.

When Mrs. Jones pulled into the driveway, Tom was waiting. He hurried out to open the van doors for the Beilers, eager for news of Jackson's condition.

He waited while Mrs. Jones and Clara decided what time she would come for them in the morning. Then Tom closed the van doors and stood back as the *Englisch* woman drove away and the four Beilers headed to the house. Lida Mae stopped and turned to him.

"Tom, my *dat* said I should help you in the barn until he gets back, probably tomorrow. Then he'll see what he can do, and I may have to keep helping you for a while."

Surprised, Tom raised his eyebrows. "*Ja?* Is he hurt bad?"

"No, thank *Gott*," Lida Mae said with feeling. "But his wrist is broken, and he won't be able to use a pitchfork or hold a lunge line for a few weeks at least. So I'll change clothes and be out to help you after I eat a bit more. I'm famished."

"No need. I finished all the chores, and the bishop's wife has the pizza in the warming oven. We were just waiting for all of you to get back. We fed Danny, though. He was too hungry to wait."

He saw the disappointment cross her face and understood she'd been looking forward to getting back to work in the barn. He'd be sure to let her have the dirtiest stalls to clean in the morning, he thought with a small grin.

"What's so funny?"

"Nothing, I was just thinking it was kind of funny that you're disappointed that you don't get to sling manure tonight. But I promise to save you some in the morning."

She returned Tom's smile. "It is kind of silly. But I can't help it. I've missed all of it, even slinging manure."

He actually understood how she felt. They stood looking at each other, and soon it became awkward. "Um, dinner?"

She nodded briskly as if pulled from a trance. "Sorry, I guess I'm not myself tonight. It's been quite a day." She smacked herself on the forehead. "*Ach!* I forgot to tell my *maem* and sisters about what happened with Danny." She bit her lip. "I hope Priscilla doesn't get angry."

"Why would she?"

"Well, I lost her son for at least half an hour. That tends to irritate a parent."

"We got him back unharmed. That should count for something."

"You have an optimistic outlook. Me? Not so much. Come on." She headed inside, followed by Tom.

Upon entering the house behind Lida Mae, he realized she'd been right about her sister's reaction to hearing what had happened that afternoon. It was hard to miss, since she immediately began yelling at Lida Mae.

"You got caught up in your stained-glass project and lost track of time, and what, forgot my son was there with you?"

Lida Mae bit her lip again and looked guilty. "*Ja*, I'm really sorry, Priscilla."

"You're sorry?" The young mother paced the kitchen while her sisters and mother, and the bishop and his wife, quietly let her work off her mad. "You're sorry? Don't you know anything could have happened? He's only five, Lida Mae!"

"But, nothing happened—" Lida Mae explained, but Priscilla had worked up a fine head of steam and cut her off.

"*Nee!* Don't lie to me! Danny told me all about it!"

"You were only in here for a minute or two before I came in. He couldn't have told you all about it," Lida Mae grumbled.

"Oh, no? He was pretty excited to share his little adventure. He said he'd been playing with toys in the workshop while you worked on your glass. It stormed, but he said he wasn't scared because Aenti Lida Mae and Blue were with him. After a while he got bored, and since the storm was over, he decided to take a walk with the dog. He crossed the orchard and went into the stud pasture with Simon and Boss. That's where you found him. Sound familiar?"

"Um…"

"But that isn't all!" Priscilla turned to her mother in an appeal. "There was a copperhead! The horse killed it, in front of my five-year-old son."

"Because he was protecting us from stepping on the snake," Lida Mae ventured.

"What if Danny had gone in that way and stepped on the snake before you got around to noticing he wasn't where you thought he was? He could have died before you ever found him!" She tossed her hands into the air, glaring at her youngest sister. "Well, you won't have to worry about losing track of my son again, because I'm not going to trust you with him anytime soon, Lida Mae." She looked around, as if suddenly realizing she had blown her top in front of the bishop and his wife, and Tom, and Danny, who was standing in the doorway to the kitchen looking teary-eyed.

"*Maem*, Simon wouldn't hurt me," he whispered. "He's a *gut* horsey. And Tom and Aenti Lida Mae kept me safe."

Lida Mae stepped toward her sister and reached out a hand. "I'm really sorry, Priscilla. I was terrified, I won't deny it. Tom and I looked all over for him. The house, the hay loft where the new kittens are. Even the stall where the Haflinger mare has her new foal. You know how Danny's been begging us to take him to see it—I thought maybe he went on his own."

Rhoda tentatively spoke up. "That's true, Prissy, he

has been asking to see that foal. And she does seem really sorry."

When Priscilla turned her angry eyes Rhoda's way, their middle sister hunched into herself and looked apologetic. "I'm just saying."

"Tom helped me search," Lida Mae added. "We knew he was safe with Blue, right, Tom?"

Tom, hesitant to intrude in a family dispute, nevertheless felt the need to assure Priscilla that Lida Mae had not taken the boy's disappearance lightly. "I've never seen Lida Mae so distraught, Priscilla," he said quietly. "And the stud horse really is very gentle…except, apparently, with venomous snakes."

"I don't care! Danny is all I have left, don't you understand? I can't lose him the way I lost his father! I just can't." Her voice broke, and she turned into her mother's arms.

"There, there, Priscilla. It's understandable you're upset. But everything turned out fine. *Gott* protected your little boy."

"And Simon," Danny chimed in, drawing smiles from a few of those listening. But Clara looked disturbed as she gazed at her youngest.

"Lida Mae, I'm quite disappointed in you. You were entrusted with the most important thing in the world—a child's safety. And you were careless with your charge, and although nothing bad happened, it could have turned out very differently, indeed."

"*Maem*," Rhoda said, "to be fair, it could have happened to any of us. We all become engrossed in our work when we're doing a project, whether it's a fabric quilt or one of our basket or barn-art quilts." She looked at Priscilla. "Be fair, Prissy. You know how it is."

Her face set and white, Priscilla shook her head. "*Nee*, Rhoda, there's no excuse. If you know you're likely to get lost in a task, then don't do that task when you're in charge of a child! Especially one that isn't your own." She looked at Lida Mae, and Tom was taken aback by the anger and sorrow in her eyes.

"Lida Mae, I love you, but I'm going to have to pray hard to forgive you."

"Priscilla," Bishop Lapp said, "perhaps enough has been said in anger for tonight." He held up his hands when he saw the young mother's eyes fill with tears. "I'm not saying your feelings are unfounded. But I think it would be *gut* for all of us to sleep on this, and maybe we could talk about it in a day or two?" He looked around the room, and everyone nodded.

"That's a *wunderbar* idea," Sally agreed sympathetically. She went over and gave Priscilla a gentle, one-armed hug. "I think everyone is quite exhausted after the day you've had. Priscilla, why don't Ben and I drive you and Danny home? We go right past your place."

Priscilla nodded stiffly. "*Ja, denki.* I'll just get our things."

Tom could see that Lida Mae was having a very hard time. Her face was pale and stricken, and she hurried over to her sister. "Please, Priscilla, don't leave angry at me! I'm so sorry, I never meant to neglect Danny. I love him, and you, so much! Please forgive me!"

Priscilla wouldn't meet Lida Mae's eyes, but she nodded. "Of course, I will forgive you, Lida Mae. *Gott* says we must forgive, and I'll probably even stop being angry in a couple days."

Lida Mae looked hopeful. "Then, you'll trust me with

him again?" she pleaded, putting a hand on her older sister's arm.

Priscilla looked down at her sister's big hand resting on her small wrist, and she shook her head. "I don't know, Lida Mae. I'll pray about it." Taking Danny's hand, she said, "I'm ready, *denki*. We just need to collect Danny's car seat from my buggy. Good night." She walked out the door without speaking or looking at Lida Mae again.

The bishop followed her, but Sally turned and patted Lida Mae's shoulder. "She'll get over it, Lida Mae. A mother's love is a very powerful thing, and she's afraid. It will be fine, you'll see." Then with a wave for everyone, she hurried outside.

Lida Mae went and stood in the doorway, watching them drive away.

Tom ached for her, but knew it wasn't his place to interfere. Clara walked over and wrapped her arms around her youngest daughter. "Sally is right, *lieb*. Give your sister a few days. She'll come around."

"*Ja*, the next time she needs a babysitter!" Rhoda joked. Lida Mae smiled at them, appreciating their support, but she still felt wretched about what had happened.

"Let's sit and eat this food the Lapps brought," Clara said. The meal wasn't as boisterous with conversation and laughter as usual, Tom noted, but he supposed everyone was exhausted. And Jackson, the heart of this family, was absent.

After supper, Tom excused himself to use the washroom while Rhoda and Lida Mae stowed the leftovers and did the dishes. While her daughters cleared up, Clara read aloud to them from her Bible.

When he returned he discovered the kitchen empty, but the back door was standing open. He went outside and found Lida Mae sitting on one of the rocking chairs on the porch. She looked up as he approached. "*Maem* and Rhoda went to bed. I thought I'd sit out here and look at the stars for a bit before I head up."

"Do you mind if I join you?"

She shook her head and he took the other rocking chair. For a few minutes they sat together in silence, each lost in his or her own thoughts.

Finally, Tom rolled his head to look at Lida Mae. "You know, I never finished what I was telling you before the Lapps got here."

She frowned at him, then her expression cleared. "*Ach*, you mean right after you laughed at me when I'd just told you how I'd gone out on a limb for you, and would have to confess my dishonesty to my parents?"

He felt a blush rise up his neck and cover his face, and was glad of the darkness. "Um, *ja*, that's when."

"I guess you might as well tell me then. Maybe I'll be able to have a *gut* laugh at your expense."

He peered at her, and could tell from her slight smile that she was joking—mostly.

"Okay, well, the thing is, I did pretty much exactly the same thing you did. I wrote to a few connections in Texas telling them what a *wunderbar* horsewoman you are, and recommending you as someone they might want to hire to improve their breeding programs."

He risked another glance at her, and saw that her jaw had dropped and she was sitting upright in the motionless chair. "You did what?"

He shrugged. "You heard me."

She opened and closed her mouth a couple of times. "I'm not sure what to say."

Now it was time to tell her the rest; the part likely to make her mad. "That's not all, though."

"What do you mean?"

He chewed his lower lip. This was the tricky part. "Well, I wanted to cast you in the best possible light, so I mentioned that in addition to your extensive knowledge about horses and skills on farm and ranch, you were a gifted quilter and artist, an experienced teacher and shopkeeper, and a gut cook and housekeeper, and that you might be interested in, ahem, finding a match—but only with a man who would appreciate your qualities as a rancher and farmer!"

He winced, certain he was about to feel the heat of her anger at that last part. But she surprised him. She sat back in her chair and recommenced rocking, staring out into the night while she thought about what he'd said. "You make me sound like quite a paragon."

"I was being honest."

After a while she chuckled. "It's worth noting that I didn't feel the need to mention your domestic skills or marriageability in my letters."

He shifted uncomfortably at this truth. "Sorry. I was just trying to…"

"Cast me in the best possible light, right." She sighed and waved it away.

"So now what?"

He frowned. "What do you mean?"

She stood and paced down the porch steps and into the yard before turning to stare up at him. "What happens next?"

He realized he hadn't thought that far ahead, so he winged it. "Well, I guess we wait to see if anyone offers either of us a job."

"And if they do, what then? We just up and leave?"

"I guess that's up to each of us. It'll depend on the job offer, and, um, other things."

"Other things?"

He didn't dare tell her that he'd all but changed his mind about leaving Ohio, and instead very much wanted to court her and eventually offer her marriage. He had to be certain that if and when their relationship changed, it wasn't because she had no other options. He wanted a life partner who loved him, not someone settling for a guy who would let her keep doing her preferred chores and hobbies.

So he didn't tell her how his feelings for her had been growing and changing until he didn't feel as if the day had begun until he caught sight of her bright smile and heard her ringing laughter.

Instead he just shrugged. "Sure. For example, we can't leave right now with your *dat* hurt. So it will depend on whether a job offer can wait. Stuff like that."

She smacked herself on the forehead. "I'm so selfish! I can't believe I forgot about my *dat*! He'll be home tomorrow, and he can't do the work he loves. I know how that feels, Tom. I can't think about leaving right now. Who knows how long he'll be unable to work the farm?"

"Right. But that doesn't mean if you get a gut offer you can't think about it. And when the time is right, you can show it to your parents, and see what they say."

"They'll say I've lost my mind, is what they'll say!"

He stood and walked down to join her in the yard, where he placed his hands on her shoulders and gave a little squeeze. "Lida Mae, you don't know your own worth. My guess is that they'll do whatever it takes to keep you here. You won't have to go anywhere. But if not, you'll have a choice, ain't so?"

Her lips parted and his eyes were drawn to them. He stepped abruptly back before temptation got the better of him. She cleared her throat and he waited to hear what she thought.

"I guess I see what you mean, Tom. But do you really think they'll want me to stay that badly?"

"Oh, *ja*, Lida Mae. I definitely do think so. If you were mine—my daughter I mean—I wouldn't let you go if I could help it."

She smiled. "*Denki*, Tom. That's a very nice thing to say." She tucked a gleaming strand of moonlit red hair behind an ear, making Tom long to reach out and feel what that shining silk felt like in his work-roughened hands. He shoved his hands into his pockets, and she continued, oblivious to her effect on him.

"So, I guess we just need to see if we get any offers. Because it might not be me who has to make a choice. It could be you."

He fervently hoped not. But on the other hand, if she didn't share his feelings, heading back out west with a *gut* job offer for himself and Jake might be the best thing for him.

"*Ja*, it could be me."

"That's what you want, right?" She studied him intently, and he wondered what she wanted him to say.

"Well... I guess it'll depend on the offer, and on whether they include Jake in it. Otherwise, what's the point? I really want to work with my *brudder*. I'd be willing to consider an offer almost anywhere to do that."

She nodded slowly, seemingly satisfied with his answer. "*Ja*, okay. So we wait?"

He caught her gaze with his own, silently vowing that in whatever time they had, he would do his best to make her feel valued and cherished. And if the day came when she decided to leave—or when he felt he must leave—he would face it with whatever grace he could muster.

His eyes holding hers, he reached out a hand to her. She bit her lower lip, but then tentatively held out her own and clasped his. He savored the feel of her warm skin, and gave her hand a small, reassuring squeeze before smiling at her. "*Ja.* Now we wait."

Chapter Eleven

Lida Mae tossed a pitchfork full of soiled bedding into the wheelbarrow outside the stall she was cleaning the next morning.

She was dressed in her barn clothes, and breathing in the scents she loved, doing work she enjoyed. It was unfortunate that the reason she was able to enjoy the work was that her *dat* was hurt, but she'd decided to separate the two things in her mind. So far, that seemed to be working for her.

She'd been entertaining herself with thoughts about Tom. She couldn't believe he'd had the same idea she had, and had acted on it in precisely the same way! "Like minds!" she chuckled. "You have to appreciate that!"

The fact was that she'd been noticing other things about Tom Fisher that she appreciated. His humor. His loyalty to his brothers, and even to the parents with whom he was presently at odds. And he was very easy on the eyes, she thought with a small giggle. It was too bad he wasn't a few inches taller. She sighed as she recalled the Amish girl waiting for him in Texas. "Forget about it, Lida Mae. You'll only get hurt again if you go there."

After finishing the last stall, she turned to push the laden wheelbarrow out to the farmyard to empty it onto the manure stack, and pulled up with a start when she saw Tom leaning against an empty stall across the aisle, a straw between his strong, white teeth, grinning at her.

She couldn't help noticing how fit he looked in his barn clothes, and she had to force her eyes back to the waiting wheelbarrow so she didn't bobble it.

"Tom! I'm glad you're here. I've been wanting to talk to you. I thought of something last night."

"What's that?"

Somewhat breathlessly she hurried to explain. "It occurred to me that I'm going to have to keep a close eye on the mail. If my *dat* were to receive an answer from one of the men I wrote to, it would be very awkward, to say the least."

"To say the least," he agreed.

She started to push the wheelbarrow toward the exit, and let out an annoyed "Hey!" when he shouldered her aside and took the handles from her and wheeled it outside to empty it on the stack in the manure storage area. She stalked after him, hands on her hips.

"What do you think you're doing? I'm perfectly capable of doing that!"

"*Ja*, I know, Lida Mae. But I was raised to be a gentleman. So when I see a woman doing a heavy task I can help with, I do, *fashtay*?"

She frowned. She knew he was only being helpful, but he was doing it in a high-handed way she couldn't abide. "*Ja*, I understand. But I need you to understand that I enjoy doing the heavy tasks that I'm basically not allowed to do anymore." She stalked up to him and planted a finger in the middle of his chest. "So do you *fashtay*?"

Raising his eyes a bit to meet hers, he said, "*Ja*, I do. Sorry. I won't make that mistake again."

She dropped her hand, unable to believe she'd poked him in the chest, although it was a very nice chest. "Look, Tom, I'm sorry. I'm on edge."

"I understand. Things are in turmoil here at the moment. If you weren't affected, you wouldn't be human. But I just want to help."

She smiled at him. "*Denki*. I'll try not to bite your head off next time."

He gave her a long look that had her shuffling her feet. "What?"

"Your *dat* will be home in a little while, right?"

Nervous about where he was going with this, she nodded cautiously. "Right. Mrs. Jones picked *Maem* up a while ago to go get him. What does that have to do with anything?"

"It just seems to me that your life would be easier if you told your *dat* what you'd done instead of worrying what he's going to do when he finds out."

She gasped. "I can't do that! Not until we see if it works! Tom, you can't tell—promise you won't!"

He looked reluctant, but he finally nodded, filling her with relief. "Okay, but only for a week. After that, we come clean. Agreed?"

The relief flipped right back to anxiety at that. "Only a week? That might not be long enough. If the men I wrote to don't answer by then…"

"Lida Mae," Tom interrupted, holding up a hand to stop her. "I'm a man of integrity. It bothers me that you've gone behind your father's back on my behalf. One week. That's all I can agree to."

Vexed, she folded her arms across her chest. "Well, what about you? You said you did basically the same thing! Where was your integrity then?"

He gave her a small smile. "I said 'basically' the same. The difference is that I didn't forge my father's name. I wrote the letters in my own name on your behalf."

She felt like a fool. "Oh. I didn't get that part."

"Look, don't feel bad. We should know our options inside a week. And maybe there are options we haven't considered."

She pondered what he might mean by that. "Other options? Like what?"

He looked uncomfortable. "I don't know. We haven't thought about them yet! So while you're watching the mailbox waiting to see whether or not you'll be able to palm me off on one of your horsey connections out west, just keep your mind open to other possibilities."

"Tom, I'm not trying to palm you off!" When he started chuckling, she realized he'd been trying to lighten the mood. She huffed out a breath. "Fine. I'll keep my mind open, although I don't know what other options there might be. I either stay here, or I leave. That's two, and I've already thought of them!"

"You know, leaving to work on someone else's spread isn't your only way out of here."

She blinked at him. "Now what are you suggesting? I'm not going to jump the fence or anything. I like being Amish."

"I never suggested such a thing! But horses aren't the only thing in the world, you know. You've got other talents and skills. And you could use them somewhere else, even if you didn't find a position on another ranch."

She pondered this for a moment, wondering why the possibility hadn't occurred to her. "You mean, like, move to another Amish community? Get a job? Huh. I hadn't even considered that. But I guess I could."

She wondered why the very idea depressed her. She looked around the farmyard, at the beautiful ranch and farm and home her parents had built. Other than a couple of visits to other Amish communities over the years for family weddings or brief vacations, she hadn't been out of Charm very often.

"I never thought of going anywhere else," she confessed in a small voice. "I love it here."

"Hey, I'm not saying you have to go anywhere. Just that if you wanted to, you could. I'm sure you have friends and relatives in other places who could offer you a job. You'd meet new people." His eyes shifted away and he added, "Maybe even a special fellow."

She wondered why he sounded a bit flat when he mentioned that last bit. She looked at him, but his face gave nothing away even as his eyes returned to hers. "You're right. I'll think about it." She heaved a sigh. "I suppose if I can't live here the way I want to, I might as well leave. It would hurt too much to stay and never be able to work with the horses."

And she realized that staying here if Tom left, even if she got to work with the horses again, had somehow lost some of its shine. When had that happened?

"If that's how you feel, then you should definitely consider your options. But remember, there are always possibilities that you might not be aware of yet."

She peered at him crossly. "Now you're the one making cryptic remarks."

He chuckled. "I'm just saying, there might be something *gut* here that you don't know is a possibility yet. That's all. Think about it. Use that excellent brain *Gott* gave you for something other than forging letters."

She rolled her eyes at him. "Okay, I'll keep an open

mind. But if you know of something I don't, just tell me. I'm not good at puzzles and games, Tom."

The look he gave her was pensive and had butterflies fluttering in her stomach, but he didn't elaborate on his thoughts. "I'll tell you when I'm certain something is an option. Not before. See you at lunch." He took up the handles of the wheelbarrow and pushed it back into the barn, leaving her alone in the barnyard staring after him and wondering what options he might be talking about that she couldn't see for herself in the plain light of day.

"Unless he knows of some tall Amish man who has recently moved to town and is looking for a stubborn wife who likes to do men's work and has what most consider an *Englischer* hobby, and he'd be just fine with all this, then I can't imagine what the infuriating man is talking about!"

Unless... Was there any possibility that Tom might return her feelings? Could he be suggesting, in his less-than-obvious way, that maybe he was a possible option for her? That the two of them could have a future together?

"Oh, *sis yuscht*! Of course not. Now you're just reading your own wishes into the situation. If the man was interested, he'd simply say so. Wouldn't he?"

Unsure, and not willing to make a fool of herself by coming right out and asking him about his feelings, she tossed her hands into the air, she headed inside to change clothes and get lunch ready. Her parents would be back soon, and she was scheduled to work that afternoon in the quilt shop.

Late that night Tom was awakened by a commotion coming from outside. His window was open to the warm summer night, and once he was fully awake he became aware of the furious screaming of horses and the barking and yipping of a number of coyotes. Obadiah's old dog, Ethel, sleeping in the kitchen, was carrying on, too, barking madly and running around the first floor to get her owner's attention.

"Oh, *sis yuscht*!" he cried, jumping out of bed and struggling into his bathrobe before throwing open her door and hurrying into the hall.

From downstairs, a sleepy voice called, "Tom, what's going on?"

Tom clattered down the stairs and thrust his feet into his boots. He grabbed the old shotgun, loaded with rock salt, from the hooks above the door. "Obadiah! Coyotes are attacking the horses! I'm going out." He started down the steps, then turned and called, "Whatever you do, do not let Ethel get outside!"

"Wait one minute for me, boy! I'm coming, too!" The old man hurried out of his room, his own feet stuffed into dirty barn boots. "Give me the shotgun! It's a cranky old thing and particular about how it's handled. You could blow it up in your face!"

With no time to argue, Tom handed over the gun and ran out onto the porch, where he saw a sight that caused his blood to run cold. Lida Mae was tearing full speed across the farmyard toward the pasture where two horses were under attack by what sounded like a large pack of coyotes. Obadiah pushed through the door, shotgun in hand. "Let's go, boy!"

As he ran across the farmyard, Tom heard Jackson bellowing from the main house, "Coyotes! There are coyotes in the pasture with the horses! Everyone up!"

Tom couldn't understand how there could be a mare and, he saw as he ran toward the paddock, her young foal, outside, since he'd personally made certain all the horses were safely inside their stalls and the barn doors shut before retiring for the night. As he ran, Obadiah huffing along behind him, he could see the two horses huddled together, the mare turning her hind quarters toward the intruders who circled around, yapping and calling, careful to stay out of range of the mare's lethal hooves while trying to get close enough to grab the young foal.

"Lida Mae, wait! We're coming!" Tom called as he ran toward the action. But Lida Mae didn't slow down, probably because, Tom figured, she'd realized the horses didn't have much time. He could see that the mare was tiring, and it wouldn't be long before the determined canines had the foal.

"Don't shoot me, Obadiah!" Lida Mae yelled as she ran. "I'm going in!"

Ignoring the old man's shout that he would handle it, Lida Mae climbed up on the fence and hopped over into the pasture, still ignoring Obadiah and Tom's cries telling her to wait.

The coyotes were becoming bolder in their determination to have the foal. Tom had just reached the gate when he saw Lida Mae drop to one knee, and carefully sight along the barrel of the shotgun, pointing at a group of coyotes off to the left, away from the horses, Tom and Obadiah. He winced at the gun's roar as it sprayed rock salt into the swirling group of canines. They immediately scattered, yipping in outrage, and ran away across the pasture. Seeing their pack mates heading for the hills, the rest of the group gave up on the horses and took off after their companions. Lida Mae discharged the other round at their retreating forms, even as Tom and Obadiah hurried into the enclosure.

Tom knew that the rock salt wouldn't do any real harm

through the thick fur coats of the small predators, but it stung for sure and certain, and the animals might decide it was easier to go after deer or rabbits next time and leave the well-protected horses alone. "Go check the horses, Obadiah. I'll make sure Lida Mae is alright."

Lida Mae had pushed to her feet and turned to check on the mare and foal, who had calmed down with the departure of the coyotes, and didn't see Tom running over. She crashed right into him, and he caught her in his arms, and found himself holding on tight, unwilling to let her go.

"Tom! Let me go, I have to check the horses!"

"Shh, they're fine. Obadiah is with them. Let me look at you."

"I'm fine! I've got a shotgun. You're not even armed!"

She pushed away and stalked over toward the horses, leaving Tom to take a few deep breaths. He'd held her and intellectually he knew she was unharmed. His emotions, on the other hand, were not convinced.

He turned and followed her. "Are you insane coming out here alone with nothing but rock salt? Do you have any idea what could have happened?"

At Tom's angry shout, the mama threw up her head and pranced a bit, whickering nervously. Lida Mae held out her hand and moved slowly, crooning gently to the mare, which was a horse Tom knew she'd helped raise from a foal. "It's okay, mama. You know me. I'm sorry about the loud bangs. The scary coyotes are gone. And the angry men will stop yelling now, right?"

Tom clenched his fists and told himself to stop behaving like a fool. Lida Mae had only done what any rancher or farmer would when her stock was in danger. But that didn't mean he'd liked being helpless while she took all the risks.

The horses soon settled as Jackson, Clara and Rhoda hurried into the paddock. A quick glance assured Tom that they'd managed to keep the dogs inside so they wouldn't try to chase after the coyotes.

Tom saw Priscilla and Danny huddled on the porch, Priscilla's arms wrapped around her small son, watching from safety in case the pack returned. He recalled that they were spending a night or two at the farm while their own house was being painted.

"Lida Mae!" Obadiah wheezed. "Didn't you hear me yelling at you? I could have handled that!"

Clara hurried up to her daughter and took the shotgun from her, handed it to Jackson and ran her hands over her daughter's face and form to be sure she was unharmed.

Lida Mae squirmed under the attention. "*Maem*, I'm fine!"

"Oh, Lida Mae!" Clara threw her arms around her youngest child. "Why did you run out here alone? You c-could have been k-killed!" She hugged her daughter fiercely before thrusting her to arm's length and shaking a finger in her face. "Next time let your *dat* handle any coyotes that show up!"

Jackson cleared his throat. "To be fair, Clara, I couldn't handle a shotgun one-armed." When she spun to look at him furiously, he shrugged. "Sorry. I wouldn't have been able to do more than jump up and down and yell. Lida Mae saved the horses."

"Well, I had a shotgun, and I could have taken those coyotes off running!" Obadiah growled. But everyone knew by the time the elderly man had reached the pasture, the foal most likely would have been caught and carried off despite the efforts of its dam.

"Why didn't you take the gun?" Jackson asked Tom.

Tom looked at Obadiah, obviously not wanting to throw the old man under the buggy, and Rhoda spoke up. "I'm guessing Obadiah wouldn't give him the gun."

Obadiah looked a bit embarrassed. "I didn't know if the pup knew how to use it. You know how temperamental it is."

Tom thought that the first thing he'd be doing in the morning would be buying his own shotgun. He couldn't take another scare like this one.

"Okay," Jackson said, letting the matter go. He looked at Lida Mae with new respect. "I don't think I've ever seen such fine shooting, Lida Mae. You saved that foal for sure and certain."

Obadiah was scratching his head in puzzlement as he regarded the horses, who were cropping the grass peacefully as if they hadn't been fighting for their lives minutes before. "What I want to know is how those horses ended up out here in the first place." He looked sternly at Tom. "Didn't you put them up before dark?" Tom nodded. "Lida Mae and I brought all the stock in before dark, like always. We made certain they were secure before closing up the barn for the night."

"We did, *Dat*, for sure and certain!" Jackson frowned. "Let's go have a look. Tom, bring the horses. Let's not give the coyotes another crack at them tonight."

"I'll be right there, Jackson," Tom said. He walked over to where Lida Mae stood with her mother and sister. "Sorry for overreacting, Lida Mae. I realize you did what you had to do; what any stockwoman would do. And you did it very well. And it's not like I would have been much use, unarmed."

Lida Mae stared at him a minute. "*Denki*, Tom. I admit I was a bit frightened, but everything happened so fast, I didn't really have time to be too scared. Do you want me to help you get the horses inside?"

"*Nee*, let the men handle it from here, Lida Mae," Clara said. "You need to come inside and get cleaned up."

"I'll see you later. I need to get the horses inside." With a nod at all of them, Tom walked over to catch the mare by her halter to lead her inside the barn, followed by her prancing foal.

As Lida Mae climbed the porch steps to where Priscilla and Danny still waited, her sister offered a tentative smile. "*Gut* shooting, sis."

Lida Mae smiled back, then her gaze went to her nephew, who was staring after Tom as he led the horses toward the barn. Following his gaze, she saw that the big sliding barn doors were standing open just wide enough for the Haflingers to slip out. She frowned, wondering how that had happened. When she glanced back at Danny, he looked away, a peculiar expression on his small face. Before she could wonder about it, Priscilla picked him up and said, "Time to get back to bed, *lieb*. It's late." She said good night, then carried the boy inside and headed upstairs with her son.

Inside, Lida Mae reassured the dogs that all was well before she hurried upstairs, shucked off the soiled bathrobe and nightgown and headed into the bathroom for a shower. She donned a clean nightgown, and Rhoda knocked on the bathroom door, a clean bathrobe clutched in her hands. "Here, I grabbed *Dat's* bathrobe. You can use it until yours is washed."

Lida Mae took the offering and smiled at her sister. "*Denki*, Rhoda."

"I'll be downstairs. I want hot chocolate and cookies before I try to get back to sleep."

Rhoda trotted down the stairs while Lida Mae pulled on her father's fuzzy brown robe, which was much too big for her. But she belted it and bloused it at the waist so it wasn't too long. It would do. As she headed downstairs, she turned a troubling thought over and around in her head, the way you might a loose tooth.

Blue came to meet her at the bottom of the stairs, and she scratched the dog's head as she walked into the kitchen.

"Sit, child, you must be exhausted!" Clara pulled out a chair, and Lida Mae sat, accepted a mug of steaming hot chocolate from Rhoda and stared at the door, waiting for the men to come inside and tell them what they'd learned.

While she waited, she silently prayed.

Denki, *Father, for giving me the courage, speed and aim to scare off those coyotes. Amen.*

But something was nagging at the back of her mind, that niggling thought she'd been wrestling with since it occurred to her in the shower. As she sipped her comforting drink, Danny's peaked little face, lined with worry as he watched the men and horses walking to the barn, drifted before her mind's eye.

Why was the memory bothering her? She was too tired to think about it. She'd sleep on it, and hopefully in the morning, she'd realize it was nothing to worry over.

Chapter Twelve

Lida Mae sorted a new shipment of colorful fat quarters at the quilt shop the next day. The cotton was of excellent quality, sure to wear well, and the colors were vivid, and should be slow to fade, making them perfect for quilts that would give years of warmth and beauty.

"Oh, you were right about these," Clara said as she picked up two different shades of violet. "They're temptation incarnate!"

"I'm going to have to make something from these." She pondered a moment, fingering the fabric as she thought. "Hmm. Maybe a spring table runner."

Realizing her mother had stopped sorting through the new fabrics, Lida Mae refocused on her parent, who was just standing there, staring at the pile of colorful fat quarters scattered across the counter.

"*Maem?* Is everything alright?"

Clara shook her head, and Lida Mae caught the glint of moisture in her normally imperturbable mother's eyes. She reached out and put a hand on her mother's shoulder, giving a little squeeze. "What is it?"

Clara shrugged and sniffled. "I… I just feel so bad, *lieb*, about everything. Your *dat* and I didn't mean to ruin your life." A quiet sob escaped Clara, and Lida Mae became seriously concerned.

"*Maem!* I know that. I won't pretend to agree with your decision, but you're my parents, and I know you love me and have only my best interests at heart."

Clara raised troubled eyes to her daughter's concerned ones. "Do you really?"

A sound, somewhere between a laugh and a sob, escaped Lida Mae, and she nodded emphatically. "Of course! I've been praying a lot for things to work out. I know they will."

Clara dug in her apron for a tissue, then blew her nose and blotted her eyes. "You're a *gut* girl, Lida Mae. You always have been. I wish that I could tell you everything could go back the way it was before, but Tom is here now, and even though I regret it, I still think I'm right about the impropriety of you doing men's work on the farm."

"When I'm married, maybe my husband will feel differently, though," Lida Mae said softly. "I've been praying for someone who will want me for who I am, not for who people think an Amish woman should be."

Clara smiled and tossed the tissue into the trash can behind the counter. "That's a wise request, Lida Mae." She frowned at the fabric, and then looked at her daughter. "I know what I said about your glass making, but the fact is, you're really *gut* at it." She shrugged. "Who am I to forbid you from pursuing an obviously *Gott*-given talent?"

Lida Mae bit her lower lip to avoid pointing out the irony of this comment, given that was exactly what her *maem* had done in regards to her farm and ranch work—at least, in her opinion.

Unaware of the direction of her daughter's thoughts,

Clara went on. "Besides, we need more stock for the shop!"

Clara looked at the spots where Lida Mae's glass creations usually hung, casting colorful refractions of light around the shop. "The customers really do love them." She picked up one of the fat quarters she'd been examining. "I think we have a lovely violet sprigged fabric that would pair well with these." She hurried off to look at the blues and purples, leaving Lida Mae smiling at her retreating figure.

She glanced up when she heard a buggy pulling up, and her eyes widened when Tom climbed down, gave Toad a pat and secured him to the hitching rail. *"Gut,"* she whispered, looking around the store, which she was glad to see was empty for the moment. "Now, I can talk to Tom about how those horses got out last night."

When her father had returned to the house the previous night, he'd been alone, as Tom and Obadiah had gone back to the bunkhouse to catch what sleep they could before the sun rose. Jackson had shaken his head in puzzlement. The mare's stall door had been standing open, as was the big sliding door leading out to the farmyard.

The horses hadn't opened them. So someone had opened the stall and barn doors, and left them open. She was sure those horses had been safely closed into their stall the night before. Or...almost sure. Now, she was beginning to doubt her own memory.

Quickly rounding the counter, she hurried to the front door, and called behind her, *"Maem!* I'm going out for a few minutes. I'll be back soon!" She didn't wait for an answer, but pushed through the door to the front porch of the shop, meeting Tom as he started up the steps.

He looked surprised, and tipped his straw hat back to

peer up at her. "*Guder mariye*, Lida Mae," he said with a smile. But when she stood there, hands on her hips, frowning at him, his smile faltered.

"Let's go for a walk, Tom. I need to talk to you."

He quirked an eyebrow but nodded and stepped back down off the steps. "Okay, where do you want to go?"

She brushed past him and started down the sidewalk. "It doesn't matter. I just want to be away from my family while we talk so they don't overhear us."

As they walked down the sidewalk, Lida Mae studied Tom surreptitiously.

Stealing a peek at his strong, clean profile, she wondered when he'd become a person to her? She pondered the question as they headed down the sidewalk, and she turned away from town and down a residential street.

About halfway down the block, Lida Mae stopped and faced Tom, folded her arms across her chest and demanded, "Okay, tell me what you and *Dat* found when you checked out the barn last night. Do you have any idea how those horses got out?"

Tom knew she wasn't going to like what he had to tell her. "Lida Mae, when I mucked out the stalls this morning I found something in the stall that was left open last night."

"You did? What is it? Let me see."

With a crooked smile on his face at her eagerness, he reached into his pocket and pulled out a small metal truck, which he handed to her.

She peered at it, then back up at him, her face troubled. "*Ach, nee*. This was in the straw you removed from their stall this morning?"

He nodded. "*Ja*. And I think we can both deduce whose it is."

Lida Mae swallowed painfully and nodded, clutching the small toy in her hand. "I'm not sure how to handle this. Priscilla is still sore at me about the other day. But I'm not surprised that you found this toy in the stall."

"You're not?"

She shook her head. "*Nee*. Last night as I was going back inside after we'd chased the coyotes away, I saw Danny looking after you men and the horses as you all walked back to the barn. He had the oddest look on his face. A cross between guilt and relief. I couldn't understand it." She dropped the little truck into the pocket of her apron and patted it. "But if he somehow let those horses out, that would explain it."

"It would. And remember, he's been asking to see that foal for weeks. Do you think he got tired of waiting?"

She grimaced. "It looks that way, for sure and certain. I'll have to talk to Priscilla about this. It's not going to be fun." She started walking back to the shop.

Tom matched her pace. "*Nee*, but he's just a *boppli*. He didn't mean any harm, and I'm willing to bet he's learned his lesson."

She nodded. "I can see him sneaking in there, but what would make him leave without securing the doors again?"

They had reached the shop, and Tom unhitched his gelding from the post. "I guess we'll have to ask him." Unable to think of anything else to say on the matter, he touched a finger to the brim of his hat. "I'll see you later."

"*Ja*, later." She paused. "And, Tom? *Denki* for telling me about the truck." She reached out a hand and he caught it and gave it a little squeeze, finding he didn't want to let go right away. His breath caught as their gazes tangled.

He found himself tugging her a bit closer, and her eyes widened in confusion.

"Tom?" She whispered the question, pulling his gaze away from her green eyes and down to the sweet bow of her lips. His own parted as he imagined tasting her, just for a brief moment. What would it be like?

Unreality seized him as he felt himself leaning in and she did nothing to stop him.

A car drove by, shattering the moment, and they jumped apart.

Lida Mae looked at the ground, and Tom took a few seconds to collect himself. "Um, sorry, I'm not sure…"

"No! Don't worry, just one of those things," she laughed nervously, her eyes meeting his briefly before darting away. "Well, I need to get back inside. So, I'll see you later."

"*Ja*, I'll pray that your conversation with Priscilla goes well."

"*Denki*. Bye." She took a few steps, then spun to face him. "Tom. I just want you to know that, whatever happens, you know, with the letters…wherever we both end up… I think you're a very *gut* man. I'm glad you're here and I've had a chance to get to know you a little."

With a final nod, she hurried toward the shop leaving Tom rooted to the sidewalk, staring after her. She thought he was a good man? After he'd shown up and, as she'd so aptly put it, stolen her life?

He wasn't as good as she was. She was kind, and generous. And really pretty. Which didn't matter, of course, as he knew better than to judge a woman by such a changeable, fleeting yardstick.

But Lida Mae didn't need to depend on her outer beauty.

She was just so…bright. So sparkly! Her personality was effervescent…at least, when she wasn't imitating a porcupine.

At some point, Lida Mae Beiler had transformed into his idea of the ideal woman. Or maybe his idea of the ideal woman had transformed into Lida Mae Belier.

He could no longer deny that he was developing feelings for her.

The only question now was, what was he going to do about it?

Chapter Thirteen

Lida Mae peeked out the front door to be sure Tom was gone. She watched him guide Toad down the road toward home, then turned and headed toward the back of the shop, where her mother and Rhoda were working on projects. She found Rhoda alone in the work area.

"Lida Mae! You're back! *Maem* and I wondered where you'd gone." She peered beyond her sister, and frowned when she saw that she was alone. "I thought Tom was with you."

"*Ja*, he was. He found something when he was mucking out the stalls in the mare's wing this morning."

"What did he find?"

"Where's *Maem*?"

"In the kitchen."

She leaned in and whispered, "He found one of Danny's little metal trucks."

Lida Mae stood back, an expectant look on her face as she waited for her sister to put two and two together. She saw the moment when the light dawned.

Rhoda's hands flew to her face. "Oh, *nee*! Lida Mae, you're not thinking…"

Lida Mae nodded. "*Ja*. And I'm not sure how to handle this, Rhoda."

Rhoda drew in a deep breath, which she held for a few seconds before letting it out slowly. "Prissy's not going to want to hear it. You need to tread very carefully, little sister."

"Tell me something I don't know!"

After a few moments, Rhoda shrugged. "Well, nothing bad ended up happening, so it's really not that big a deal, is it?"

"No, but it could have been. Nearly was. That foal is valuable, and the mare could have been badly hurt, too."

Rhoda frowned. "Well, I'd say talk to him, see if he'll confess. Then have him tell her himself."

Lida Mae pondered the suggestion. "That's a really *gut* idea, Rhoda."

Rhoda smiled wryly. "I occasionally have one."

"That is, assuming I can get a few minutes alone with him."

"They're staying again tonight. Their house still isn't painted. It should be finished by tomorrow, though."

Lida Mae considered this, and then nodded. "Okay, then, I'll have a word with him when we get home tonight. It's got to be eating him up. I'm surprised he hasn't come forward on his own, actually."

"For sure and certain. He must really be scared."

"I'll try not to frighten him further. But if he did this, he needs to confess it, for his own good. Not to mention, making my life a whole lot easier than if I have to confront Priscilla."

Rhoda picked up her needle and squinted while she threaded it. "You're not kidding!"

Lida Mae and Rhoda were putting the finishing touches on dinner that evening when the sound of a buggy in the driveway caused both women to stop their work for a moment.

Lida Mae hurried to look out the kitchen window. "That's Priscilla's buggy. Okay, so the plan is that after dinner you suggest to Priscilla that she help you with the dishes while I go out and help with the evening barn chores since *Dat* still can't do them."

Rhoda added, "*Ja*, and then I'll 'notice' that you forgot your barn gloves."

"Which I'll leave right on the chair by the back door," Lida Mae continued.

"And then I'll ask Danny to run them out to you in the barn."

Lida Mae nodded. "At which point, I'll show him the truck, and get his story if I can."

The back door opened, and Danny ran into the room. When he caught sight of Lida Mae and Rhoda, a troubled expression crossed his face, but he turned away and muttered something about playing with his farm toys and disappeared into the living room.

Priscilla and Clara followed at a more sedate pace, laughing about something. When they saw that Rhoda and Lida Mae had dinner on the table, Clara smiled. "*Ach!* How nice. Let me ring the dinner bell and get the men in here." She stepped back out onto the porch and rang the triangle, then returned inside and closed the door.

"I'll have time to wash my face and hands before we eat. Where did my grandson go?"

"He's in the living room, *Maem*," Rhoda answered, putting a platter of meatloaf onto the table.

"Danny, come wash your hands," Priscilla called, walking to the sink and turning on the water. She washed her own hands, and helped Danny climb up onto a stool to do the same.

The back door opened, and Obadiah, Tom and Jackson entered.

"Mmm, meatloaf, my favorite!" Obadiah said with an appreciative glance at the table.

"Wash your hands, everyone, then we can eat!" Rhoda said as she placed a bowl of brown buttered noodles and another of stewed tomatoes onto the table. Everyone soon found their seats, and Jackson led the family in a silent mealtime prayer. Then they began passing the platters and bowls around and filling their plates. The conversation ranged from what was happening at the quilt shop to rumors of a budding romance between two *youngies* in their district to last night's unsolved mystery of how the horses got out.

Lida Mae stole a glance at Danny when that topic was raised, and noticed that the boy was not eating.

His mother noticed as well, and smoothed his hair. "What's wrong, Danny? You love meatloaf."

Danny shrugged, but didn't answer.

Looking concerned, Priscilla felt his forehead. "You're not getting something, are you, *lieb*?"

Oh, nee, Lida Mae thought. *All we need is for him to be sent to bed early, and ruin our plan!*

Rhoda must have had the same thought, because she quickly chimed in, changing the subject to the next weekly livestock auction to be held on the following Wednesday in Mount Hope. "I was thinking it would be fun to get a llama," she said, erasing any thoughts of last night's adventures in everyone's minds.

"What?" Obadiah said around a mouthful of mashed

potatoes. "We don't need one of those fussy critters. Did you know they spit at people they don't like?"

As talk turned to the pros and cons of llamas, Lida Mae cast a grateful look at her sister, who winked when nobody was looking.

After dinner, the plan went off just as they'd hoped. The men got up from the table and Jackson headed into the living room with Obadiah to talk a bit before bed.

Tom headed to the barn, accompanied by Lida Mae, who threw a glance at Rhoda to be sure she remembered to carry out her part of the scheme. Priscilla and Rhoda were clearing the table as Lida Mae left.

"Is something up?" Tom asked as they walked side by side into the barn.

"Rhoda and I worked out a plan to get Danny to confess," Lida Mae told him.

"Really? What's the plan?"

Lida Mae smiled when a small voice called her name. "Aenti Lida Mae? You forgot your gloves!"

Tom cocked an eyebrow. "Part of the plan?"

"I had to get him out here away from his *maem*. I'm winging it from here."

"Want me to stay, or go?"

"Stay. He likes you."

Danny ran into the barn, Lida Mae's gloves clutched in his small hand. "There you are. Aenti Rhoda told me to bring you your gloves."

He handed them to her and was about to turn and run back to the house when Tom stepped forward and spoke to the lad. "Hey, Danny, since you're out here, why don't we go back and take a look at that foal you've been wanting to meet?"

Lida Mae cast an approving look his way, impressed with his quick thinking.

Danny looked unsure. "I'm not supposed to stay out here and get in the way, *Maem* said."

"You won't be in the way. And I know you've been wanting to see that foal," Lida Mae said with a smile. "Come on."

She led the way through the barn to the broodmare wing, and soon they were standing in front of the stall containing the horses that had gotten out the night before. Danny looked miserable, standing there shuffling his feet, not looking at the horses.

"Is something wrong, *lieb*?" Lida Mae asked gently, putting a hand on her young nephew's shoulder.

He shook his head, still not meeting her eyes. So she dug into the pocket of her apron, pulled out the little truck and showed it to the boy.

"My truck!" Danny cried. "I lost it last night when I..." His words dried up, and he swallowed hard. He darted glances at Tom and Lida Mae, and looked as if he was going to either burst into tears or run away.

Hoping to head off tears, Lida Mae gave his shoulder a squeeze. "It's alright, Danny. We know it was an accident. Why don't you tell us what happened?"

Big tears started leaking down Danny's face, and he sniffled and swiped the back of his hand across his nose. "I didn't mean to let them out!"

Lida Mae met Tom's eyes over the boy's head. "Of course, you didn't, *lieb*."

Between hiccupping sobs, the story came out. Danny had grown tired of all the grown-ups forgetting their promises to take him to see the horses. He knew he wasn't allowed in the stables alone, but he was determined to see that foal. So he'd waited until everyone was asleep, and then he'd snuck outside with a flashlight. He'd had no trouble with the well-oiled and balanced sliding barn door. The stall door had given him a bit more trouble, but by standing on a small crate, he'd managed to unlatch it.

"The mama horse didn't mind me coming in to see her baby," he said earnestly, looking at the mare who was standing placidly while the foal nursed. "She likes me. So does the foal."

"Of course, they both like you, Danny," Lida Mae said. "What happened to make you leave without securing the stall door?"

The boy's expression turned frightened. "I heard coyotes! They sounded close. So I ran back to the house and upstairs into my bed. I... I thought I pulled the latch on the stall closed, but I guess I didn't. I'm sorry!"

He started crying again, and Lida Mae gathered him up in her arms. "Shhh, *lieb*. It was an accident, and nobody was hurt."

"Danny? Are you the one who let the horses out?"

Tom started at the voice, coming from just outside the stall where he saw Priscilla had been standing, unnoticed for who knew how long. He realized she must have overheard some of Danny's confession.

At the sound of her sister's voice, Lida Mae spun around and gasped. "Prissy!"

"I didn't mean to, *Maem*!" Danny cried, hurrying to his *maem* and burying his face in her skirt.

"Oh, *lieb*," Priscilla murmured, "I know you didn't."

"I'm a bad boy!"

Priscilla's hand flew to her mouth as tears filled her eyes.

"*Nee, nee*, you're not, Danny," Lida Mae murmured.

"Everyone makes mistakes. *Gott* knows this and loves us, anyway."

Tom saw Lida Mae's eyes meet her sister's as she spoke, and Priscilla nodded. "*Ja*, everyone makes mistakes, and I made one for sure and certain."

"You mean because Danny got out without you noticing?" Lida Mae asked, no sign of irony or malice on her face; only love for her sister and nephew.

Priscilla smiled. "That, too. But I was referring to the other day, when I accused you of not paying attention to my son. Obviously, you were right. It could happen to anyone."

She kissed Danny on the head and turned. "I'll see you both later. I need to get this boy to bed."

She carried the tired child out of the barn, and Tom sent up a silent prayer of thanks for the way the scene had unfolded between the sisters. Then he stole a glance at Lida Mae, and found her staring back at him, a peculiar look on her face.

"What?"

She shook her head, looking away. "Nothing." Then she looked frustrated, and she took a deep breath and looked him in the eyes. "Tom. You've been so *gut* through all of this. You were kind last night to Obadiah when he wouldn't let you have the gun, even though you're much younger and faster. Many people would have been angry and cruel, but not you."

"What would be the point?"

She planted her hands on her hips, and he bit back a grin at her fierceness. "Would you please let a person compliment you?"

He gave a graceful gesture. "Please continue."

"You could have handled the situation with Danny

differently when you found the truck, and made things worse. But you didn't. It's obvious you care about people. We're blessed to have you here."

Her formal tone left him frustrated. He'd come to crave something a bit more personal from this woman. Taking a step closer to her, he brushed a lock of hair back behind one ear and smiled into her eyes. "Those are nice words, Lida Mae, but I would have done those things for anyone. It's called being a decent human being."

"Oh."

"But this time, it felt different."

She blinked at him, and he felt a surge of affection for her.

"Different how?"

He put a hand on either side of her waist, and tried to convey his feelings for her through the tender look he gave her. "I wasn't thinking of anyone except you."

"You weren't?"

He drew her a little bit closer. "Only you, and about how I could make your life better through my actions."

She swallowed and her eyes dipped to his lips before jerking back up to look into his. "Why would you be thinking about me?"

At her whispered question, his heart melted. He could see her feelings reflected in her beautiful eyes, and they filled him with hope. He placed one hand on the back of her head and drew it down slowly until their lips were nearly touching before answering softly, "Because I see you, Lida Mae. Only you."

With that he closed the distance between them and brushed his lips over hers in the gentlest of caresses. Then he let his forehead rest against hers.

"I need to tell you something."

"I'm listening."

"I've come to care for you, Lida Mae. It snuck up on me, probably because of your regularly delivered insults and reminders that you couldn't wait for me to go back to Texas."

"Hey! You weren't exactly Mr. Charm, either."

"Maybe so. I've never been very smooth with women. And I was kind of a hot mess when I got here. All I could think about was how my whole future had been stripped from me without my consent, and I was so bitter. I was so focused on going backward to what I used to have, that I almost missed out on moving forward to what I could possibly build here."

"You're sounding pretty smooth now, Tom."

He smiled into her eyes again. "I'm having a hard time remembering why it seemed so important for me to return to Texas. I hope you'll give me a chance to show you how I feel."

He drew back and looked at her. "That is, if you have feelings for me, too?"

She paused a moment, as if considering his question, and he felt the first stirrings of alarm. But then she placed a hand on his cheek and murmured, "Let me show you," before softly returning his kiss.

After a blissful moment, their lips parted, and Tom opened his eyes and found her watching him nervously, as if afraid of what he would say.

"So, I guess that means you do have feelings for me?"

She gave a breathless laugh. "It seems I do. They snuck up on me so gradually I didn't even realize it was happening. But I think I had my first inkling when you told me you'd written to some of your connections about a job where I'd be appreciated for my skills with ranching and farming."

His smile widened. "Really? I knew I had feelings for you before that."

"Oh, *ja*?"

He nodded. "I think it was when I watched you creating your stained glass that night after the CPR class. You were so competent and so obviously passionate about your work there, just as you are with the horses. I found myself wishing that you felt that same way about me."

"You mean like you were a project I needed to work on?"

His eyes crinkled with amusement. "I guess that's one way of looking at it."

Before she could answer, the sound of a throat being indignantly cleared, had them jumping apart as if burned. They both turned to look into the corridor outside the horse stall, and found Jackson glaring at them, eyes narrowed. He lifted a hand, in which he held several letters, and Tom's stomach dropped as he realized what they probably were.

"Oh, no. I forgot to check the mail today," Lida Mae groaned quietly.

Tom's fears were confirmed when Jackson peeled two of the letters away from the others and offered them to him.

"If you're finished handling my daughter," he bit out, "you might want to read these. They look important."

Tom accepted them wordlessly and looked at the return addresses. He closed his eyes a moment before stealing a glance at Lida Mae, whose face was nearly as red as her hair.

"*Dat*, this isn't what it seems."

Jackson turned a wry look on his youngest daughter and gestured at her and Tom. "Oh, I think I know what *this* is." He shook the remaining letters, which he had opened and presumably read, at her. "These, however, I don't understand."

He pulled out one of the letters and skimmed the contents before raising his eyes to Lida Mae's. "This is from James Yoder in Oklahoma. He writes that he's impressed with my desire to help my employee—that's you, Tom, in case you didn't know—find work closer to his home in Texas, and also by Tom's extensive experience and qualifications." He snorted and stuffed the letter back into its envelope before pulling out the other one and shaking it open.

Tom met Lida Mae's eyes, and his heart hurt to see the panic and sorrow she was obviously feeling at disappointing her father.

Jackson continued. "This one is from Rick Sanchez in New Mexico." He looked up at Lida Mae. "You remember Rick. He's got that really nice spread where he breeds mostly Palominos." To Tom he explained, "We stopped there on the same trip when we visited your family."

"*Dat*, please, let me explain," Lida Mae started, but Jackson held up a hand. "Rick writes that he's surprised that I'm willing to let such a wonderful employee go, and he also thinks I'm a really great guy for helping you out this way, Tom. He also says that any cowboy or farmhand I personally recommend is good enough for him, and he'd love to have you join his outfit." He replaced the second letter into its envelope and leveled a look at his daughter and Tom. "The funny thing is, I can't remember writing to either James or Rick. Maybe my concussion made me forget."

Tom cleared his throat. "Jackson, this is my fault, not Lida Mae's."

"*Nee! Dat*, it's my fault! I treated Tom so badly from the moment I met him that I decided I needed to make amends by helping him get back home. Or at least as close as possible."

"So you wrote to my colleagues and signed my name pretending to be me?" He looked outraged.

"Well, *ja, Dat*. Like I've done many times before, only those times were at your direction. So they recognized my handwriting and thought it was you." She heaved a deep breath, and Tom saw the sparkle of unshed tears in her eyes. "I know it was wrong, and I'm sorry. I was just trying to help Tom because his parents are being so unfair. Please forgive me, *Dat*. I can't stand for you to be angry with me."

Jackson blinked at Lida Mae and looked at the letters in his hand. After a few moments, he nodded slowly and returned his gaze to his daughter. "I see what you're saying. You really have been a huge part of this farm's success for years." He gave a humorless laugh. "I even had you writing my letters. You probably know as much about running this place as I do. And I guess what you didn't say was that it isn't only Tom's parents who have been unfair."

He looked at Tom, who found it hard not to turn away from the pain and guilt he saw in the older man's eyes.

"Well, you might as well open those, then and see what they say."

Hoping for a reprieve, Tom ventured, "That's okay, I can look at them later."

Jackson smiled, somehow making him feel even worse. "I'd appreciate it if you opened them now, son. Since the two of you have been more or less plotting behind my back, I think you owe me that much, don't you?"

Lida Mae gasped, and Tom saw that the tears she'd been fighting had escaped and were rolling down her cheeks.

Feeling extremely small, he nodded. He tore open the first envelope, from a farmer in Texas who raised American Paint horses and Clydesdales. He wasn't Amish, but he was a fair man Tom and his family had dealt with for years. Glancing through the man's response to Tom's query about work for Lida Mae, he felt a surge of pride as he saw that the man was offering her a good paying job helping to run the breeding side of his operation, all based on Tom's recommendation.

"I see from your expression that you've received good news, ain't so?"

Tom recalled himself, and said, "I guess so, *ja*."

"Go ahead and open the other one then."

Tom looked at Lida Mae, hoping for guidance, but she merely stared hopelessly back at him, her expression one of misery.

He tore open the other letter, this one from a rancher in Wyoming, and saw that Lida Mae could have her pick of two good jobs should she decide to leave Ohio. He looked at Jackson and said, "More good news."

Jackson nodded. "So with these two, that makes four job offers for you back west, young man. I'd say you've got your pick. *Gut* for you. I know you never wanted to come to Ohio, and I'm only sorry that I was a party to forcing it on you." He handed the two letters in his hand to Tom, and turned to look at his daughter. "Well, it looks as if you'll get your wish, daughter, at least for now. With Tom leaving, I'll have to tell your *maem* that I need you back on farm and ranch duties. I hope you're satisfied with the way you brought this about. I'm not sure I could be if I were you. But then again, I guess we did put you in a pretty untenable situation, so part of the blame, at least, rests on your *maem* and me."

"Wait, *Dat*! It's not like that. I know I should have asked before writing to your associates. It's just that I wanted to help Tom, and I was afraid..."

Jackson waited a moment, then pulled a hand down his face and over his beard. "You were afraid I'd refuse. And why wouldn't you think that, given my apparent lack of care for your feelings recently?" He looked at Tom, bewilderment in his eyes. "If you'd told me you were that unhappy, I would have helped you. I thought you were coming to like it here."

He turned to look at Lida Mae. "I forgive you, Lida Mae. I just need a couple of days to figure out what to do about this."

Tom couldn't stand by any longer, letting Jackson misunderstand the full implications of the situation.

"Jackson, wait. These two letters weren't about me."

Jackson gave Tom a puzzled look. "Not about you? Then who? Your younger brother, the one missing an arm?"

"*Nee*, Jackson. I'm sorry. When I saw how much Lida Mae wanted to do ranch and farm work, I realized I could help her find a place where she would be appreciated for who she is, not just as a woman, but as an expert horsewoman. So I wrote to my connections in Wyoming and Texas, and they've both offered her a job in their horse breeding operations."

Lida Mae gave another gasp. "Really? Oh, help! I can't believe it!"

Jackson looked from one of them to the other, a frown on his handsome face. "So, you both wrote to connections on each other's behalf? Was this something you cooked up together?"

"*Nee*, Jackson, we both did it independently, and only found out we'd both done it after the fact," Tom explained.

Jackson looked at Lida Mae, who nodded. "That's what happened, *Dat*." She let out a sob, and covered her mouth with her hands. "But I don't really want to leave! I just want to be able to do what I love here!"

Tom held his breath, praying that Jackson would accept his daughter's plea for forgiveness—and for love and acceptance of who she was.

Jackson blinked a couple of times and then opened his arms. "Come here, Lida Mae," he said gruffly.

With a glad cry, Lida Mae buried her face against his chest. Tom could tell she was crying, and Jackson patted her awkwardly on her back, murmuring "there, there" while looking helplessly at Tom.

A distant voice from down the long corridor of the brood mare barn interrupted the moment. "Jackson? Lida Mae? Where are you?"

"*Maem!*" Lida Mae gasped, wiping at her face. "Oh, *sis yuscht*. She's going to be so angry at me!"

Jackson gave his daughter a last squeeze and released her. "We're going to have to tell her that the two of you are leaving us." He pulled an enormous white handkerchief from his pocket and swiped it across his eyes before blowing his nose like a foghorn. He frowned mightily, then sighed. "I reckon you'd better let me handle it. She's going to be very upset."

He hurried out of the stall. "Give me a few minutes before you come back inside. And no more kissing! As if we didn't have enough to worry about." He strode away, but they heard him call back, "And remember to fasten that stall door securely!"

Tom and Lida Mae stared at each other for several heartbeats, before Lida Mae said in a small voice, "Upset is an understatement of what *Maem* is going to be."

They listened to Jackson greeting Clara at the end of the corridor, and his booming voice carried back to them as he explained that they'd be along in a bit, and that he was ready for bed. Their voices faded away, and there was silence.

Tom cleared his throat. "So. *Are* we both leaving?"

Lida Mae gave him a stricken look. "*Ach*, Tom. I just don't know what to do. I can't believe I actually have a choice!" She spun away and clasped her hands to her chest before spinning back to face him, a look of joy on her beautiful face. "It's just amazing that both those outfits want to hire me—*me*—to work with their breeding programs!"

Tom felt a smile spread across his face, though he was torn between his happiness for her and his need to grab on to her and tell her that she didn't have to go anywhere to be wanted for herself—he wanted her just the way she was!

But he knew he couldn't do that. He understood that she had to make up her own mind, and while he could make it clear to her that one choice was that she could spend the rest of her life with him, it was now only one of several options for her.

And he wasn't at all certain that he was such a good catch that she would give up the tempting offers she'd received to become his *fraa*, even if it did mean she would still be able to do the ranch and farm work she loved, at least when he could afford his own spread.

You've got no one to blame for this situation but yourself, Tom! You're the one who had the bright notion to send those letters off to your colleagues. You've made your bed, as the saying goes.

He smiled at her sadly, and she returned his look, the joy melting off her face. "I guess we both have some thinking to do, ain't so?"

He nodded. "That we do. But I'm happy for you, Lida Mae. Whatever you decide, I'll be your biggest supporter."

"And you, Tom. Now you can go back out west, if it's still what you want to do."

She reached out a hand, and he caught it. He ran a thumb over the calluses she'd earned through years spent tossing hay and mending fences, riding horses and repairing tack, and wondered how he could have ever preferred some dainty, soft-handed girl to this amazing woman.

"Come, we'd better go inside and face the music." She tugged his hand and together they walked toward the farmhouse where the rest of her family waited.

Chapter Fourteen

Lida Mae dragged herself through the breakfast routine the following morning, assigned to setting the table and putting out dishes prepared by others after she burned a dozen eggs she was scrambling because she was too tired to focus.

Her *maem* hadn't mentioned the letters or job offers, and when Lida Mae tried to talk about it, Clara had shaken her head. "*Nee, lieb.* Wait until later, after breakfast."

Lida Mae had gotten little sleep the night before. When she and Tom had arrived back at the house after their discussion with Jackson, they had found that everyone had gone up to bed. There was a note on the table from Jackson saying he and her mother would talk to her in the morning.

Tom had returned to the bunk house without giving her the goodnight kiss she had secretly been hoping for.

Before he'd left, though, he had handed her the two letters containing job offers. She had made herself a cup of tea and taken it and the letters up to her bedroom, where she'd read them each several times before turning off the battery-powered lamp on her bedside table.

All night long she had tossed and turned, alternating

between prayers for guidance and wondering what she should do.

And the one question that loomed largest in her mind wasn't about her future career prospects. It was much more personal than that.

Her first thought upon waking had dragged her right back into that internal debate. What did she really want? And did it even matter? Tom had not mentioned marriage the previous day. She'd thought long and hard about that during the endless night.

He mentioned having feelings for me, but that's not a marriage proposal. Oh! I wish I'd come right out and asked him what he wanted. I might have gotten more sleep.

Finally the meal was ready, and Danny rang the dinner triangle, calling the men in to eat.

Obadiah came in first, and Lida Mae was surprised to see that Rebekah was with him. "*Guder mariye*, Rebekah, Obadiah!"

"Good morning to you, Lida Mae," Rebekah replied as Obadiah poured himself a cup of *kaffi*, and a second one for her. The healer peered closely at Lida Mae. "You look tired. Are you feeling well?"

Lida Mae sipped her own *kaffi*, and mustered a smile. "*Ja*, I just didn't sleep well. A lot on my mind."

The back door opened and Jackson and Tom came inside, leaving their work boots on a mat by the door. Lida Mae's breath caught when she saw that Tom looked as tired as she felt. So he'd also spent a restless night! He turned and gave her a soft smile, and suddenly the morning seemed brighter, and she breathed a little easier. Maybe everything would work out.

"I thought I saw your buggy, Rebekah!" Jackson

boomed. "What brings you here so bright and early?" He sniffed the air and frowned. "From the smell of things, I hope it isn't breakfast."

Clara snapped a tea towel at her husband and told him to wash up and have a seat. "We had a little issue with the first batch of eggs, but I promise you won't go hungry, husband."

He laughed and followed Tom to the sink. Once they'd taken their seats and prayed, they passed the food and loaded up their plates.

Lida Mae was trying to think of a way to get Tom alone so they could talk about what they were going to do when Obadiah cleared his throat. She looked up and found the old man smiling around the table at them all, a beaming Rebekah seated beside him, holding his hand. Lida Mae's thoughts immediately turned away from her own problems as she felt happiness blooming in her chest for her friends. She clasped her hands under the table, eyes wide.

Oh! Can this be what I've been hoping for?

"Well, this old woman simply won't leave me alone. She keeps coming over here and making up flimsy excuses to see me. The fact is, I've realized she just can't get along without seeing my handsome face at least once every day."

Rebekah feigned outrage, swatting Obadiah on the arm. "Oh! You're being ridiculous. Just tell these folks our news."

He smiled at her fondly, and Lida Mae knew her prayers had been answered. Obadiah confirmed it when he grinned at everyone and said, "Okay, then, I asked her to marry me and she said yes! So what do you think of that!"

Everyone cheered and clapped for the elderly couple.

"This is just wonderful!" Clara cried, jumping up to hug them both. "I insist on hosting your wedding here. Obadiah is family, and you practically are, too!"

"The sooner the better," Obadiah said. "I'm not getting any younger. We'd better not push our luck."

Rebekah huffed out an exasperated breath. "Oh, you." She looked around the table. "We're going to talk to the bishop after breakfast. We'd like to get married next month." She looked at Clara, tears misting her eyes. "And *denki* for offering to host the wedding. We accept gladly!"

"Where will you live?" Rhoda asked as she grabbed a piece of toast from the platter on the table and slathered it with molasses.

"Obadiah will come and live in my house," Rebekah said. "We'll have plenty of room there, and he can help in my garden."

"Never too old to learn something new, I guess," Obadiah said, giving his bride-to-be the sweetest smile Lida Mae had ever seen on his weathered face.

Tom smiled fondly at the older couple. "Congratulations to you both! I'm so happy for you!"

Talk turned to wedding plans, and after breakfast Obadiah and Rebekah left to talk to the bishop and Priscilla and Rhoda hustled Danny out the door to drive into town and open the quilt shop.

"*Maem* said she needs to talk to you about something," Rhoda murmured to Lida Mae as she placed her black bonnet over her white prayer kapp. "Are you in trouble or something?"

Lida Mae grimaced. "Or something. I'll tell you later, okay?"

"Better you than me, little sister." With a laugh, Rhoda hurried outside to join Priscilla and Danny in the buggy, and soon there was no one left in the kitchen but Tom, Lida Mae and her parents.

Clara set a fresh pot of *kaffi* on the table and sat down. "Well, Lida Mae. What are you going to do?"

"First, I'm going to apologize to you and *Dat* for going behind your backs and sending those letters. It was wrong of me. I'm truly sorry."

Clara nodded. "Apology accepted. And here's one from me." She sucked in a breath, and blinked back sudden tears. "Oh, *sis yuscht*. I thought I could do this without turning into a watering pot."

"Here, Clara." Jackson handed his wife a fresh white handkerchief, which she accepted with a wobbly smile.

"Denki."

She got herself under control and looked at her youngest. "Now then. I am so very sorry for not realizing how important farming and ranching are to you, Lida Mae. I've tried to force you into a mold you don't fit, and would never have been happy in. As of now, you have my blessing to return to helping your *dat* on the farm and with the horses. And I hope you can forgive me, my *lieb*."

Lida Mae's eyes flooded with tears and she cried, "Of course I can forgive you! I love you!" She hugged her mother fiercely, and saw her father pulling another handkerchief from his pocket and dabbing at his own moist eyes.

"What about me, Lida Mae? Can you forgive me, too? I had a better understanding than your *maem* of what farming and ranching mean to you." He regarded her through troubled eyes, awaiting her judgement.

"Oh, *Dat*, of course I forgive you, too. I love you, too. So, I can really come back to the barn?"

Her parents nodded, and she felt a glow of happiness.

But then she caught Tom trying to slip from the kitchen, and called, "Oh, no, you don't, Tom Fisher! Come back here and face the music with me."

He turned, a guarded look on his face. "I was only trying to give you some privacy. It's kind of a family moment, ain't so?"

She stared at him for several moments, and she thought she recognized something in his eyes that reflected what was in her heart. She turned to her parents. "*Maem*, *Dat*, *denki* so much for this. I won't disappoint either of you."

"Then you're staying?" Jackson looked as if he were afraid to hope, so she nodded. "*Ja*, those job offers made me feel really *gut*, but the truth is that I don't want to leave our home. I'm staying."

"Oh, thank You, *Gott*!" Clara cried. "I thought I'd pushed you away forever! Your sisters will be so relieved."

"Wait, they know about this?" Lida Mae asked, surprised that her parents had confided in her sisters.

"*Ja*, of course. We're a family," Clara said. "Your *dat* told us all last night, but then he shooed us all to bed and said we'd work it out today. I didn't get any sleep at all!"

"Neither did I," Lida Mae said. She looked at Tom again.

I need to figure out the rest of this with him before talking to my parents anymore. I owe it to him, whether he wants a future with me or not.

She stood. "Tom, will you walk with me? I want to go down to the pond and see if there's any watercress."

They walked silently across the fields until they reached the farm pond where Lida Mae and her sisters liked to come and dream under an ageless old willow tree. She sat on the grass at the pond's edge and arranged her skirts comfortably, slipping her bare feet into the cool water, and he sat down beside her. "Do you see any watercress?"

She shook her head. "*Nee*, it's actually a little late in the year for it. There's some here, but it'll be bitter due to the heat. That was just a ploy to get you to come down here with me. It's a *gut* place for talking."

"Ah. Well, then." He kicked off his boots, removed his socks and rolled up his pants before sticking his own feet into the pond. "Ahh, that's nice." After a few minutes spent simply enjoying the fine day and the cool water on his feet, Tom said, "I guess since you're going to be allowed to work with your *dat* again, that means I'd better take a hard look at those two job offers. Maybe one of them would take Jake on, too."

Lida Mae turned to stare at Tom, and he felt a lump form in his throat at the sadness on her face.

"So you've decided to leave?" She turned and stared out at the water while waiting for his answer.

He swished his feet around in the water, wanting to shout that he didn't want to leave. He wanted to stay and court her and marry her and build a family and a future with her. But not knowing how she felt made that impossible. After all, the night before they may have talked about having feelings for one another, and they may have exchanged a couple of innocent kisses, but nothing had been said about marriage.

He glanced at her, and she looked positively despondent. Perversely he found his own spirits rising in response. *Well, that's a* gut *sign—if she didn't care about me, she wouldn't look sad at the idea of me leaving, right? I should just come right out and ask her!*

But he wasn't quite confident enough to do so yet. So he tested the waters a bit first.

"I figure you'll be wanting me to get out of your way so you can get back to your old routines around here." He glanced at her, then studied a redwing blackbird perched on a bobbing cattail in the shallows.

"How do you figure you'll be in my way if you stay?"

Tom thought Lida Mae sounded kind of irritated.

"Well, if you're back to doing your old job, you don't need me," he offered reasonably.

"Even if Obadiah wasn't leaving, he's mostly retired. If you don't stay, we'll need to hire another person. Maybe two more, to be honest. We're growing and *Dat* and I can't keep up. I've been telling him that for a while; I just didn't expect him to fire me when he brought you in!"

He caught his breath. "Are you still mad at me for that, Lida Mae?"

She shook her head hard enough to set her *kapp* strings swinging. *"Nee!"* Heaving an exasperated sigh, she turned to face him. "Look, Tom, I need you to just come right out and tell me how you feel—about staying here, and about me. I've told you before I'm not good at games."

He chuckled. "I was just thinking I wished I had the nerve to do that. And now I find out it's what you've wanted all along!"

"Well, *ja*, Tom. I'm a pretty straight-talking woman. I'll leave you in no doubt how I feel; at least I will once I'm sure you're not going to reject me if I lay my heart out there."

"Aha! So you want me to take all the chances, is that it?"

She had the grace to laugh at herself. "I guess so. But I've given you enough reason to expect a positive response, if you choose to lay your heart out there." She gave him a lopsided grin. "So, what do you say?"

"Okay, Lida Mae, here's what I say. I say I don't want to leave Ohio after all. I say I want to stay right here, if your *dat* will have me. And I say I'm in love with you, and I want to marry you and start a family and a future with you. So, now what do you say?"

His heart in his throat, Tom waited for Lida Mae's answer to the most important question he'd ever asked.

She blinked her eyes rapidly, and then a huge grin split her face. "So, to be certain I understand, you're saying you do want to marry me even if I'm not the last Amish girl in Ohio?"

He threw his head back and shouted with laughter. "Oh, *ja*, that's what I'm saying, Lida Mae! So what's your answer?"

She batted her eyelashes at him in a fair imitation of something she'd once seen one of her sisters do, and replied, "Well, Tom, in that case, I guess I'd have to say yes, I'll marry you, even if you're not the last Amish man in Texas!"

"Yes!" He pulled her into his arms and hugged her, rocking her back and forth for several moments before pulling back, capturing her face in his hands and putting all of his feelings into a kiss that lingered. When they pulled apart, Tom tucked a loose strand of copper-bright hair behind her ear.

"I have to think that since we're unofficially engaged, your *dat* wouldn't object to us kissing once in a while."

"I wouldn't be too sure of that!" She fanned her face and he laughed again, feeling absolutely marvelous. He climbed to his feet and grabbed her hands, pulling her to hers. And they shared another sweet kiss under the willow tree before picking up their shoes and socks and walking together hand in hand back to the house to tell her parents.

Only one thing worried him, and he decided to come right out with it this time instead of living in an agony of suspense. "Do you think I'll be able to stay on here as a hand?"

"Oh, I think so."

"Really?"

"Really. I know the owner, you see. He listens to my opinions. And I intend to tell him that we need to hire your *brudder*, Jake, too. I hear he comes highly recommended."

Hope surged in his chest. It would be amazing to be able to call Jake and tell him he had a job here on the same spread as Tom if he wanted it.

"That would be *wunderbar*."

Suddenly she stopped walking and turned to him, a look of uncertainty on her face. Whatever was troubling her, he wanted to make it right. He squeezed her hand. "What's wrong, *lieb*?"

She nibbled on a thumbnail and gave him a sheepish smile. "I just want to be certain you're doing what you really want. I don't want you settling. If your heart calls you back to Texas, I think I might be able to live there with you, even if it is arid and hot. What matters to me is being with you, Tom. Everything else is secondary to that, now."

"I'm certain, Lida Mae. Ohio has grown on me, even if it is cold and snowy."

She laughed. "It must be 95 today in the shade!"

He held up a finger. "But, it will be cold and snowy in a few months, ain't so?"

"This is true. And it'll be too late for you to back out by then, so be really, *really* sure."

Lida Mae wasn't sure why she was giving Tom a chance to change his mind. *Not very bright, missy!*

She only knew that her feelings for him were so strong, it would break her heart to marry him if his heart wasn't similarly engaged.

But he quickly set her mind at ease.

"I promise, I am sure. Really, *really* sure." She chuckled and he continued. "The fact is, I've changed since coming here. I'm not the man who arrived here, full of anger and resentment. I've learned a lot here, Lida Mae. I guess you could say I've grown up. Mostly, I've learned what's really important to me. And even though I miss my family, it's not in Texas. It's right here."

She sighed, capturing his other hand and holding them both. "You don't care that I'm taller than you are? Or that I wear boy's clothes when I work on the farm? Or that I make stained-glass art? Or that I sometimes have a bit of a temper?"

"I don't care about any of that. As long as you don't care that I'm shorter than you. Or that I might try and push my Texas ways of doing things on you. Or that I can be stubborn and mulish from time to time."

"I don't care about any of that," she said.

"So then, you haven't changed your mind? You want me to stay?"

"Oh, *ja*, please do." Smiling at him, she snuggled her head onto his shoulder and wrapped her arms around him.

He held her close, and she heard him whisper a little prayer. "*Denki, Gott*, for sending me here to find this amazing woman to love, even when I was stubbornly insisting that I wanted to go back to Texas."

Smiling, she whispered a prayer in turn. "*Denki, Gott,* for letting my parents send for this wonderful man for me to love, even when I was insisting that I wanted him to go back to Texas. You know best. And as always, You got it right, despite us."

"I think we should go inside and tell your parents I want to stay here if they'll let me. And ask your *dat* for permission to marry his baby."

"They'll be thrilled on all counts, Tom."

"How do you know?"

"Because, they want me to be happy. And you make me happy."

"You sure have changed your tune in the last couple of weeks!"

"Don't remind me of the things I said to you before! You're not the only one who has grown up, Tom."

"I liked you before, and I love you now." He leaned down to steal another quick kiss, but a loud throat-clearing had him and Lida Mae jumping apart guiltily.

"Didn't I say no more kissing? Unless, of course, you two have a question to ask your *maem* and me?"

"Oh, *Dat*!"

"Don't 'oh, *dat*' me, missy. Come inside. Your *maem* and I have been waiting long enough." To Tom he said, "Parents like to be asked a thing like this, young man. That would be before the kissing." He turned and went inside, letting the screen door bang shut behind him.

"Well, that actually sets my mind at ease a bit," Tom confessed.

"What do you mean?"

"I was afraid he would kick my *hinnerdale* all the way back to Texas for daring to look at his baby girl."

She laughed aloud. "We proper Amish *maedels* frown on violence. I won't let him."

She squeezed his hand. "Come on, Tom. Let's go get our future started." They walked together to the house, where Lida Mae knew her parents would open their arms and lives to Tom, and probably to his brother, too.

For the first time in a long while, she felt hopeful and optimistic about her future.

Gott really was very, very *gut*!

* * * * *

Dear Reader,

Thank you so much for choosing my first Love Inspired story! I love writing about strong, independent women who fall for men confident enough to let their heroines shine. If you enjoyed Lida Mae's story, you might be interested in reading her sister Rhoda's story next. I think you'll enjoy getting to know the tiny, dark-haired firebrand whose heart was broken when her fiancé left her for another woman! And just wait until you meet Rhoda's adorable yellow Lab, Zoe!

I'd love it if you followed me on Facebook, and please check out my website, AnneBlackburne.com. You can sign up for my monthly newsletter, where you'll learn what I'm writing next, and what author/reader events I'll be attending. For a list of my previous Amish romances, please Google Anne Blackburne books. Thanks so much for welcoming my characters into your life!

Gratefully,
Anne Blackburne

Get up to 4 Free Books!

We'll send you 2 free books from each series you try PLUS a free Mystery Gift.

FREE Value Over **$25**

Both the **Love Inspired®** and **Love Inspired® Suspense** series feature compelling novels filled with inspirational romance, faith, forgiveness and hope.

YES! Please send me 2 FREE novels from the Love Inspired or Love Inspired Suspense series and my FREE gift (gift is worth about $10 retail). After receiving them, if I don't wish to receive any more books, I can return the shipping statement marked "cancel." If I don't cancel, I will receive 6 brand-new Love Inspired Larger-Print books or Love Inspired Suspense Larger-Print books every month and be billed just $7.19 each in the U.S. or $7.99 each in Canada. That is a savings of 20% off the cover price. It's quite a bargain! Shipping and handling is just 50¢ per book in the U.S. and $1.25 per book in Canada.* I understand that accepting the 2 free books and gift places me under no obligation to buy anything. I can always return a shipment and cancel at any time by calling the number below. The free books and gift are mine to keep no matter what I decide.

Choose one:
- ☐ **Love Inspired Larger-Print** (122/322 BPA G36Y)
- ☐ **Love Inspired Suspense Larger-Print** (107/307 BPA G36Y)
- ☐ **Or Try Both!** (122/322 & 107/307 BPA G36Z)

Name (please print)

Address   Apt. #

City   State/Province   Zip/Postal Code

Email: Please check this box ☐ if you would like to receive newsletters and promotional emails from Harlequin Enterprises ULC and its affiliates. You can unsubscribe anytime.

Mail to the Harlequin Reader Service:
IN U.S.A.: P.O. Box 1341, Buffalo, NY 14240-8531
IN CANADA: P.O. Box 603, Fort Erie, Ontario L2A 5X3

Want to explore our other series or interested in ebooks? Visit www.ReaderService.com or call 1-800-873-8635.

---

*Terms and prices subject to change without notice. Prices do not include sales taxes, which will be charged (if applicable) based on your state or country of residence. Canadian residents will be charged applicable taxes. Offer not valid in Quebec. This offer is limited to one order per household. Books received may not be as shown. Not valid for current subscribers to the Love Inspired or Love Inspired Suspense series. All orders subject to approval. Credit or debit balances in a customer's account(s) may be offset by any other outstanding balance owed by or to the customer. Please allow 4 to 6 weeks for delivery. Offer available while quantities last.

Your Privacy—Your information is being collected by Harlequin Enterprises ULC, operating as Harlequin Reader Service. For a complete summary of the information we collect, how we use this information and to whom it is disclosed, please visit our privacy notice located at https://corporate.harlequin.com/privacy-notice. Notice to California Residents – Under California law, you have specific rights to control and access your data. For more information on these rights and how to exercise them, visit https://corporate.harlequin.com/california-privacy. For additional information for residents of other U.S. states that provide their residents with certain rights with respect to personal data, visit https://corporate.harlequin.com/other-state-residents-privacy-rights/.